Wish for a Witch

First published in Great Britain in 2018 by Simon & Schuster UK Ltd
A CBS COMPANY

1 3 5 7 9 10 8 6 4 2

Simon & Schuster UK Ltd
1st Floor, 222 Gray's Inn Road
London
WC1X 8HB

www.simonandschuster.co.uk
www.simonandschuster.com.au
www.simonandschuster.co.in

Simon & Schuster Australia, Sydney
Simon & Schuster India, New Delhi

A CIP catalogue record for this book is available from the British Library.

PB ISBN: 978-1-4711-6093-6
eBook ISBN: 978-1-4711-6092-9

Printed and bound by CPI Group (UK) Ltd, Croydon, CR0 4YY

Simon & Schuster UK Ltd are committed to sourcing paper that is made from
wood grown in sustainable forests and support the Forest Stewardship Council,
the leading international forest certification organisation. Our books displaying
the FSC logo are printed on FSC certified paper.

KAYE UMANSKY

Wish for a Witch

Illustrated by
ASHLEY KING

For Poppy

PICKLES' RULES
OF CUSTOMER SERVICE

1. BE FRIENDLY
2. PRETEND THAT THE CUSTOMER
IS ALWAYS RIGHT
3. BE A GOOD LISTENER
4. KEEP PEOPLE CHATTING
5. BE SYMPATHETIC
6. USE A SOOTHING TONE WITH
THE TRICKY ONES
7. ALWAYS BE HELPFUL
8. STAY OPEN WHENEVER POSSIBLE
9. ALWAYS HAVE A HANDY HANKY
10. USE FLATTERY
11. DRAW ATTENTION TO A BARGAIN
12. NEVER SHOW SURPRISE
13. NEVER SHORT CHANGE
14. BE EFFICIENT
15. USE THE HARD SELL ONLY
AS A LAST RESORT

MAGENTA SHARP'S THREE
RULES OF WITCHCRAFT

1. Read Instructions
2. Follow Recipe
3. Make It Work

It Helps to Have the Knack.

Chapter One
MAY DAY

It was May Day in Smallbridge. The sun shone, bunting fluttered against a blue sky and the air smelled deliciously of sausages!

Smallbridge was, unsurprisingly, a small town with a small bridge. That was as exciting as it got. Fun events were rare, so all the stops were pulled out for May Day.

The whole town had turned out for the occasion. Children tugged at grown-ups' sleeves, begging for pennies to spend on sweets and toffee apples, and everyone had big smiles on their faces. The climax of the day's events would feature a speech from the mayor (long), a maypole dance from the nursery school (tangled), a puppet show (funny) and a clown (unfunny), all rounded off with a firework display (noisy!).

But right now it was late morning and everyone was gathered in the main square, where the band was playing jolly dance music. They called themselves the Smallbridge Boys even though the youngest 'Boy' (banjo) was sixty-two and the oldest (accordion) ninety-three.

Dancers filled the square – some in pairs, some in groups and some going it alone. Shopkeepers, farmers, baker boys, dairy maids, old folk, little kids, the odd daft dog – everyone was at it! Hands clapped, skirts twirled, boots

stamped, tails wagged . . .

And in the midst of it all was Elsie Pickles, wearing her best outfit and a pair of pretty blue shoes with ribbons. She had been dancing all morning and there was no sign of her feet getting tired. Dancers came and went, but Elsie danced on.

There was a reason for this. It was her shoes. Those pretty blue shoes. You see – *they had been given to Elsie by a witch!*

It happened like this.

Elsie's mum and dad owned a small, shabby shop called Pickles' Emporium. Just a few months ago, something strange had happened. A witch had appeared in the shop and made Elsie an offer she couldn't refuse.

The witch's name was Magenta Sharp, though the town knew her as the Red Witch, because she had auburn hair and always wore red. Magenta rarely came to town, and when she did, people gave her funny looks, crossed the street to avoid her, then spent days gossiping about her. Everyone said that she lived in a mysterious tower in Crookfinger Forest that could *move about*. No one really knew what she got up to there, but were sure if they did, they would disapprove of it.

I mean. You only had to look at her. Stalking about in that red get-up. Too snooty to wear black rags and

a pointy hat, like a *proper* witch. Living alone in the forest in a tower you couldn't find. It wasn't respectable.

Magenta had offered Elsie the job of tower caretaker for one week in return for a bulging purse of gold. Despite her dad's best efforts, Pickles' Emporium was deep in debt and Elsie had three hungry little brothers. So the promise of extra money was too good to turn down. Plus, after all the gossip, she had been curious to see what the mysterious tower was really like and have a real-life adventure!

The tower itself had taken some getting used to. As well as possessing

some interesting magical features, it seemed
. . . *aware*. Elsie could sense it watching and
listening. Sometimes it even gave little tremors
of approval or disapproval. There was also a
rather grouchy raven, Corbett, who Elsie had
to look after. He wasn't afraid of telling people
exactly what he thought!

Over the week, Elsie had got to know
Magenta's odd neighbours and even tried a
little magic herself. There had been squabbles,
giggles, cake eating, tears, late nights and
trouble with a love potion. Elsie had loved it!
She hadn't meant to get involved with the *witchy*
side of things but she had got sort of *sucked* in
and found, to her surprise, that she was rather
good at it. She had a knack, Magenta had said.

When the week was up, Elsie had returned
home in quiet triumph with the purse of gold, a

surprise gift of the blue shoes and the ability to do three little spells!

Now, months on, life was back to normal. Although a *better* normal than, well, normal. The Pickles had been able to pay off debts and smarten up the shop with a coat of paint, a new bell and a posh new sign. Elsie's dad had even treated them to new aprons to wear which said 'Pickles' Emporium – Where Customer Service Comes First!'

The shop still offered the same range of cheap, boring stuff – brooms, buckets, string, soap and ugly china ornaments. But now everything was displayed on freshly-painted shelves and neatly labelled. Despite the improvements, the customers still moaned. But some things never change. In order to sell things, you have to be good with people, and Elsie was. She knew the rules of Customer Service by heart.

But, oh dear. Elsie found normal life quite boring now. Shopkeeping and helping look after her brothers, Arthy, Toby and baby Todd, just wasn't enough. She borrowed books from Smallbridge's tiny library, but reading about

other people's adventures wasn't quite so exciting after having had one of her own. Sometimes she would sneak down to the stockroom and spend a few minutes practising the magic she'd learned.

The three spells she had mastered were simple, but effective. She could:

1. Produce eggs from thin air.

2. Conjure up frogs.

3. Create tiny storms in teacups.

Elsie had a feeling that her dad suspected she was up to something. He must have heard the little croakings, the rolling of eggs on the floor and the tiny rumbles of thunder coming from the basement. But he didn't say anything. What father would begrudge his daughter a little magic in her life?

But now May Day meant there was finally some excitement in Smallbridge! Elsie had been saving the pretty blue shoes for a special occasion. The second she slipped them on, she knew they were magical. Her toes tingled, energy crackled up her legs and suddenly all she wanted to do was dance!

The band was showing no signs of flagging. They struck up with the ever-popular 'Big Barn Stomp' and everybody rushed to form a circle. Elsie, pink-cheeked and bright-eyed, moved to join in . . .

And found herself rooted to the spot. Her feet simply refused to obey her.

Then, to her alarm, she was swivelled in the opposite direction, propelled forward and forced to push through the crowd, muttering, 'Sorry,' and 'Excuse me,' and 'Pardon me, was that your foot?'

The moment she was through the throng, the shoes picked up pace and took her skipping briskly back over the bridge, away from the square.

Only one pair of eyes watched her go. They belonged to the town's stray dog. His name was Nuisance, and he had been lying under the sausage stall all day, hoping that someone might drop a tasty morsel. As the small, blue figure of Elsie Pickles went tripping away unwillingly into the distance, he climbed to his feet and trotted off in her wake.

Chapter Two
THE WITCH AGAIN

The main street was deserted. All the fun was happening back in the square.

Feeling silly, Elsie skipped over the cobbles in the wayward shoes. She tried giving them orders: 'Stop, shoes!' and 'Slow down this minute!' and one or two other things she wouldn't say in front of the customers. But the shoes had a mind of their own.

A tethered goat looked up in surprise as Elsie pranced helplessly past. Chickens scattered out of her way. Behind, the sound made faint and tinny by distance, the band played on.

Pickles' Emporium was situated down a dark, narrow alley, and it was there that the shoes took her. The CLOSED sign was up, of course. Elsie's family were out having fun along with everyone else.

But someone was waiting. As Elsie approached, a tall figure detached itself from the shadows, moved forward and raised a red-gloved hand.

Elsie's shoes came to an abrupt halt.

'How do you find them?' enquired the Red Witch, peering down. No, 'Hello, Elsie.' No,

'Lovely to see you again.' No, 'How are you?' None of that. Magenta Sharp was not known for her people skills.

'Lively,' gasped Elsie. 'Hello, Magenta. It's wonderful to see you.'

And it was. All of a sudden, it looked as though life might be about to get a whole lot more interesting.

'I sprinkled them with Pep-Up Powder,' said Magenta. *Put a Pep in Your Step.* One of my bestselling products. Popular with postmen.'

'Well, it certainly works.' Elsie pointed to the sign. 'You do know we're closed? Was there

something you wanted?'

'You. I need you to deal with the mail order.'

Magenta ran a business called Sharp Spells on Tap. Sadly, it didn't live up to its catchy name. She got behind with the orders, mixed them up, wrote addresses in an angry scrawl that no one could read, forgot to put stamps on and ignored all the complaints that came pouring in from cross customers.

'Everything's out of control,' she went on. 'The office is a tip and I can't make up the spells because I've run out of all the basic ingredients. This piece of nonsense arrived too; I only read it this morning.' She reached beneath her cloak and withdrew a brown, official-looking envelope. 'It's from the Magic Board. They're threatening to take my licence away, of all the cheek.'

Elsie took the envelope and unfolded a single sheet of paper.

'This is dated three weeks ago! And you've only just read it?'

'Yes, well, I don't like the brown ones. It says

they've received a record number of complaints. Mostly about spells not turning up. Or arriving late.'

'So I see,' said Elsie, running her eyes down the letter.

'Ludicrous, isn't it?' said Magenta. 'All because a few things get lost in the post and sometimes I'm just not in the mood. Is that my fault?'

'You've been given one month to get the business in order. That's only a week from now!'

'Ridiculous. I shall object.'

Elsie shook her head. 'That won't help. It says here they've got a grade system. One is outstanding, two is good, three is requires improvement and four is inadequate. They've created a new rating just for you. Five: appalling.'

'All right, so I've got into a bit of a mess,'

conceded Magenta. 'But I can't make up the orders until I've got the stock. I'd write a list but I can't find a pencil. The complaints drawer is so full I'm thinking of taking them out and burning them.'

'Don't do that,' said Elsie. 'If you burn complaining letters, people will complain.'

'What am I supposed to do?'

'Write apologies and promise to replace the goods or give them a refund.'

'Oh, I can't be bothered with all that.' Magenta flapped a dismissive hand. 'I don't have time to write to a load of whingers.'

'But then they won't buy from you any more and you won't make any money.'

'I don't make any money anyway. They never pay up.'

'That's because they're unhappy with the

service,' explained Elsie. 'You have to keep customers happy. You give them what they want, they pay you. That's how business works.'

'Well, I'm fed up with it. It's a bore.'

'Why do it, then?'

'Well, obviously, because the world needs my amazing products. So I need an assistant and that's you. Starting tomorrow.'

'That's very short notice,' said Elsie. 'Dad needs help in the shop, you see . . .'

But inside, she thought, *Yes! Oh, yes! I'll do it!*

'So? He can hire someone. I'll pay you, of course. I take it he wouldn't object to another purse of gold?'

No, thought Elsie. *He certainly wouldn't.*

But I wouldn't do it for the money. I'd do it for the magic.

'Exactly,' said Magenta, reading her mind. She added, 'I see you've still got that dog.'

'Sorry?'

'Your dog. The one about to come round the corner.'

Elsie looked up the alley and, sure enough, Nuisance came trotting into view. He bounded up, wearing his best hoping-for-a-biscuit face.

'He's not actually mine,' said Elsie, patting his rumpled head.

This was true. But Nuisance loved Elsie. He'd followed her into Crookfinger Forest when she spent the week at the tower and now he liked to stay close to her. At night, he slept in the shop doorway. But he would never come in. He was an outdoor dog.

'I suppose he'll tag along,' said Magenta. 'I'll ask the tower to get in some dog biscuits.'

Nuisance gave a little woof. He only recognized a few words – *shove off*, *gerroutovit*, *perishin' nuisance* – things like that. Biscuits was one of the better ones. *Sausage* was best of all.

'Look,' said Elsie, 'I'll see what my par—'

'Good, that's settled. The same arrangement as before. Bring your toothbrush, walk into the forest and follow your nose. We'll find you.'

'Last time I was lost for ages before you found me,' Elsie reminded her.

'Last time I had other things on my mind. This time, I'll be watching. See you in the morning.'

And she vanished! One moment there, the next, gone!

Elsie wished she could do that. Eggs, frogs and tiny storms were all very well. But appearing and disappearing in the blink of an eye – now, that was a trick worth knowing. She could be in the library in an instant. Have a quiet read and be back in time to help give the boys their bath. Just like that!

Nuisance gave another little woof.

'Wait there.' Elsie produced a key from her pocket. 'I'm going to change out of these shoes – it turns out they can't be trusted. Then we have to find Mum and Dad. And I'll buy you a sausage.'

Nuisance changed his hoping-for-a-biscuit face into a wild-about-sausages face.

Elsie unlocked the door, hurried in and ran upstairs to put on her sensible boots. The plan was to go back to the square and tell her parents that she was off again tomorrow. She would buy a toffee apple, feed the sausage to Nuisance, listen to the mayor's speech, watch the babies' dance, see the puppet show, endure the clown and enjoy the fireworks.

Then, tomorrow, the *real* fun would begin.

Chapter Three
THE TOWER AGAIN

The sun was coming up as Elsie walked out of town with Nuisance at her heels. She had risen really early, to avoid having to put up with more fuss. Persuading her mum and dad had actually been quite easy this time. Another purse of gold would be more than welcome. Also, her dad in particular was aware that his only daughter was interested in all that 'mumbly-jumbly stuff' that she messed about with in secret and could tell she was excited to go back to the tower. But like all parents, they were full of advice and warnings and reminders, and Elsie had heard them all already so she decided to leave before they were awake.

Crookfinger Forest grew to the edge of town – vast, wild and ancient. The townsfolk avoided it. There were rumours about what was in there – wild boar, wolves, rough woodcutters who didn't wash, probably poisonous snakes and, of course, that Red Witch woman.

The first time that Elsie had ventured in, it had indeed been rather daunting. There were no paths to follow and she had got lost. But she hadn't stayed frightened for long. She soon saw the forest for what it really was: just another place where people lived. Not the kind of people who lived in Smallbridge, but people just the same.

And now, here it was again. Waiting for her, just like before. Except—

'Yoo-hoo! Elsieeeee!'

Two figures were standing under the trees, waving madly. One was a plump, pink-faced girl in a weird green dress with red toadstools on it, a daisy chain encircling her frizzy hair. At her side was a mop-haired, cheerful-looking boy with a postbag. He wore an official postman's cap, backward.

'Sylphine!' shouted Elsie delightedly. 'Joey!'

She broke into a run. The three friends fell into each other's arms and danced around in a circle, Nuisance barking at their ankles. That went on until Sylphine tripped over her dress and fell into a bush.

'Her Witchiness said you were coming,' said Joey, hauling Sylphine up. 'We thought we'd come to meet you. Hup you come, Aggie.'

'It's *Sylphine*,' said Sylphine crossly, brushing leaves and small insects from her gown. 'How many more times?'

'Well, I'm glad you did,' said Elsie. 'I've missed you.'

And she had. She'd become good friends with Sylphine Greenmantle (whose real name was Aggie Wiggins but who liked to dress in wafty gowns like a wood sprite and had invented for herself a wafty name to match) and Joey the post boy during her last stay at the tower. She was thrilled to see them again.

'So,' she said, as they set off under the trees. 'Catch me up on the news. How's Corbett?'

'Moulting,' said Sylphine. 'We asked if he

wanted to come and meet you, but he's feeling under the weather.'

'Under the *feather*, you mean,' sniggered Joey.

'What about the Howler Sisters?' asked Elsie.

'Still hanging around looking for things to steal,' said Joey. 'Last week they made off with Her Witchiness's washing line and two more buckets. She wasn't happy.'

'And what about Hank and the boys?' Elsie stole a look at Sylphine, who went pink. Sylphine had had a huge crush on Hank the woodcutter, which had caused no end of problems.

'Who knows?' said Sylphine. 'I don't like him now. Not since he got that awful haircut.'

'Hair today, gone tomorrow,' sighed Joey. 'Once Rapunzel, now Baldy the Clown. So sad.'

'How are the animals, Sylphine?' asked Elsie.

Sylphine thought of herself as Good with

Animals. Her garden was packed with bird feeders, drinking troughs, scratching posts and lots of encouraging little signs inviting the local wildlife to come and take advantage of the facilities. Sadly, animals were not Good with Sylphine. She made them nervous so they only showed up when she wasn't around. Occasionally, she managed to keep one for a pet, but it was only a matter of time before it escaped.

'Well,' said Sylphine, 'I haven't seen the tortoise for days. The fox got out and

'both the ferrets ran off. So did the hare.'

'Running a race with the tortoise, probably,' said Joey with a smirk.

'But I still have this little one!' Sylphine reached into her pocket and withdrew a tiny mouse. It sat on her palm, looking as adorable as only small mice can. 'Isn't it a darling? It's called Sweetums.'

Sweetums opened its little mouth, bit Sylphine hard on the thumb, leaped out of her hand and shot into the undergrowth. Nuisance tried pouncing on it, but missed.

'Ow,' said Sylphine, sucking her thumb.

'Fangums would be better,' said Joey. 'Here, take my hanky to mop up the blood.'

'Magenta said the tower would find me,' said Elsie as they moved deeper under the trees. 'Do you think she's forgotten? Because last time, I wandered around for ages. Sometimes she gets distracted and forgets— *What?*' Joey was poking her in the ribs.

'Behind you,' said Joey, pointing. 'Tower ahoy!'

And sure enough, there it was. Standing at the edge of a sun-speckled glade that Elsie was sure hadn't been there a moment ago. Straight, tall and ivy-covered, with the red flag fluttering from the top. Just like the last time, it had arrived quietly out of nowhere.

Magenta Sharp stood in the doorway, a shaft of sunlight lighting her red dress like a flame.

'What kept you?' she said abruptly. 'Never mind, come on in. There's cake.'

★ ★ ★ ★

There was, too. A magnificent cake stood on the kitchen table, with WELCOME, ELSIE written on the top in blue icing.

'I suppose you all want a slice?' sighed Magenta, never a great hostess.

'Yes, please,' chorused Joey and Sylphine. Outside, curled on the step, Nuisance's ears pricked up.

'Tower?' said Magenta. 'Plates and a knife, please.'

Instantly, a drawer shot open. Five plates came whizzing out and arranged themselves neatly on the table, followed by a kitchen knife that made everyone duck before landing, quivering, in the cake.

'Thank you,' said Magenta. The tower gave a

little shiver of acknowledgement.

Elsie knew that Magenta wouldn't have baked the cake. Food here came ready-made, courtesy of the tower. All you had to do was knock three times on the larder door and ask, remembering to say thank you. But still. It was a nice thought.

'Where's Corbett?' she asked, staring around. The raven's perch was unoccupied. Beneath lay an ominous scattering of black feathers.

'Well, a lot of him is there,' said Magenta, pointing. 'The rest of him is out. Doesn't want to be seen, and I'm not surprised. He's hideous.'

'I'll have to see him some time.' Elsie stuck her head through the open window. 'Corbett?'

From the shadow behind the water barrel came a feeble rasp.

'What?'

'Come and say hello,' said Elsie.

There was a pause. Then, in a flurry of feathers, Corbett flapped onto the windowsill.

He was moulting all right. There were bald patches everywhere – particularly in the head region. He wore a tiny red scarf in a vain attempt to hide it, but his scrawny neck had not a single feather left. His beady eyes darted from one face to another, daring anyone to laugh.

'There you are!' cried Elsie, Customer Service Rule Twelve coming automatically to her rescue: Never Show Surprise. Do not comment on anything the customer is embarrassed about. Ignore the boil on the nose, the droopy eye or the awful haircut. Act normal, and they just might buy something.

'See what I mean?' said Magenta, who had no such skills. 'Hideous.'

'Ah, belt up,' muttered Corbett. Which wasn't at all up to his usual standard. Normally, he would come up with a carefully crafted, bird-themed curse. *May cuckoos nest in your hideous hair. May seagulls gob on your horrible hat.* Something like that. But not today. All the fire had gone out of him.

'It's not that bad,' said Elsie kindly. 'I like the little scarf. Poor Corbett. How are you feeling?'

'Lousy,' said Corbett. He gave a weak little cough, and one of his few remaining

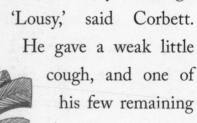

tail feathers fell out.

'Well, it won't last for ever. You'll be back to your handsome self in no time. Come on in and have some cake.'

'Mind where you land,' said Magenta. 'We don't want you shedding all over the table.'

The cake was delicious, but Magenta clearly wasn't in the mood to sit around chatting. Joey left to start on his post round. Corbett retired miserably to his sick perch. Sylphine hung around hoping for another slice, but Magenta soon put her right.

'You need to go away now,' she said. 'Elsie and I have things to do. Come on, Elsie, I'll show you the office.'

'You won't like it,' warned Corbett dourly.

He was right.

'It's a bit of shambles,' said Magenta, opening the door.

Elsie's mouth fell open. She'd been shocked at the state of the office when she stayed the first time, but now – well, words failed her.

She was facing a vast, soaring mountain of . . . everything. There was a desk and a chair in there somewhere, but they had been engulfed by all the other stuff. Books, cardboard boxes, rolls of brown paper, unopened packages (some leaking), broken lamps, a globe, a cracked crystal ball, unwashed mugs, balls of string, a dartboard. Up and up rose the mountain to the ceiling.

The peak was crowned with a snow of unopened letters. Clearly, Magenta had emptied out the complaints drawer.

'I admit I've let my standards slip a little,' said

Magenta, sounding slightly guilty for once. 'I suppose I should offer to stay and help . . .'

'No, no,' said Elsie, who thought things might run more smoothly if she was left on her own. 'I'm sure you've got other things to be getting on with.'

She was talking to thin air. Magenta had vanished again. Just like that.

That is such a useful trick, thought Elsie. *I really wish I knew how to do that...*

But right now, there were more urgent things to do. She took a deep breath, rolled up her sleeves and began.

Chapter Four
FRANK

'Oh!' said Magenta. It was the following morning and she stood at the office door with Elsie at her side. 'Well, well. That *is* impressive.'

'Thanks,' said Elsie. She felt quite proud of herself.

'Whatever time did you go to bed?'

'I didn't. I worked through the night. Once I started I didn't want to stop until it was done.'

Elsie had indeed worked wonders. The mountain was gone. In its place a tidy desk now stood in the middle of the room, with a chair tucked neatly beneath. On it was a pile of apology letters ready to be sent out to complaining customers. The books were back on the shelves. The rolls of brown paper and cardboard boxes were stacked in a corner. The floor had been swept and the window polished. Five bulging rubbish bags were piled by the door.

It looked like a regular office, apart from a tall, mysterious object draped with a dust sheet propped in a corner.

'I've made a list of the outstanding orders,' said Elsie, producing a piece of paper from her pocket. 'There are quite a lot.'

'Go on, then,' sighed

Magenta. 'What?'

'Five pots of Pep-Up Powder.'

'Ah. Brilliant stuff. You know that from your shoes.'

'Seven bottles of Squeeze 'n' Freezem spray.'

'Also highly popular. Stops people in their tracks. One squirt and they're rigid. Mind you, it only works with the right voice. You shout, "*Freeze!*"'

'That's it?'

'That's it. You could do away with the spray altogether, actually, and just shout. But people like sprays.'

'Three family-sized jars of Last Word Lozenges.' Elsie looked up.

'You know when you have an argument and

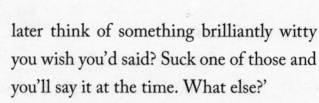

later think of something brilliantly witty you wish you'd said? Suck one of those and you'll say it at the time. What else?'

'Five vials of Yes Drops. I know what those are. You tried to get me to give them to my dad.'

'And you wouldn't. You missed a trick there. Three drops in tea and people will say yes to anything. Great fun at parties.'

'Maybe, but you can't use magic on your family.'

'*You* can't. What else?'

'Eight tubs of Cleverclogs Pills. What do those do?'

'Take daily after meals and you'll know a lot of facts and give clever speeches using long words. The side effect is you lose all your friends. No one likes a big-head. It's in small print on the

tub, but nobody reads it. Anything else?'

'Someone called Mr Eric Smalldon wrote a nice letter asking for a jar of Sharp's Hot Back Rub.'

'Right.' Magenta snatched the list and stuffed it in her pocket. 'Well, I'm out of everything. That means a trip to the Sorcerer's Bazaar. What a bore. Always a shocking queue. You have to watch the serving elves like a hawk. They put their fingers on the scales.'

Elsie was shocked. That sort of thing wouldn't be tolerated in Pickles' Emporium.

The Sorcerer's Bazaar, though. It was a fabulous name.

'What's it like?' she asked curiously.

'Just a shop. It sells everything you need. In the magical sense, obviously. You wouldn't go there for kettles or corkscrews.'

The sort of dull things we sell in the Emporium, she means, thought Elsie. And then felt a bit guilty.

'Exactly,' said Magenta, reading her mind. 'Your father is a man of no imagination.'

'He's selling what people need,' argued Elsie.

'What *Smallbridge* people need. The Bazaar caters for a different sort of customer.'

'Where is it?' asked Elsie

'Oh, way off in the seventh dimension. I'll go tomorrow.'

'Go today,' said Elsie firmly. 'The customers are waiting.'

'Let them wait. Today is Special Offer Monday. The place'll be besieged by goblins buying one spell for the price of two.'

'That's not right,' frowned Elsie. 'It should be two for the price of one.'

'They're goblins, they haven't worked that out. I can't possibly go today.'

'The letters are going out this morning promising to fill the orders within three working days. We really need those ingredients,' insisted Elsie.

'All right, all *right*! Actually, I've just had a thought. I'll ask Wendy Snipe. She buys in bulk, so there's always plenty in her storeroom.'

'Who's Wendy Snipe?'

'Wendy the Wise Woman of Clackham Common. We went to school together. Never stops talking. Awful cook. I'm certainly not staying for lunch.'

'Well, it's worth eating horrible food if you get the ingredients today,' said Elsie. 'Oh, before you go. I came across an old mirror under the dust sheet. What shall I do with it? It looks out of place, now everything's neat and tidy.'

They both stared at the shrouded shape in the shadows.

'Dump it,' said Magenta. 'It came with the tower. It was occupied by a very annoying genie once, but I'm pretty sure he's gone. Stick it out back by the privy for the Howlers to steal. They can admire their tails in it. Right, I'm off. If I go now, it'll be too early for lunch.'

And she was gone. Just like that.

Elsie looked around at the tidy office. 'What do you think, Tower?' she asked the empty room. 'Am I doing a good job?'

The tower gave a little shiver of approval. Elsie smiled. It was good to know that it was on her side.

'Elsie?' came a voice from below. 'Where are you?'

'Up here,' called Elsie. 'Room with the red door.'

Footsteps came slapping up the stairs. Once or twice, they stumbled. Sylphine, of course, in one of her silly, trailing dresses. She appeared in the doorway a bit puffed out, closely followed by Joey.

'I was just passing and thought I'd show you my new gown,' panted Sylphine. 'What do you think?' She gave a clumsy twirl, knocking over one of the rubbish bags by the door.

'Very nice,' said Elsie. 'Very . . . pink.'

'Her Witchiness popped up out of nowhere and said there were letters to post,' said Joey. 'Can we come in?'

'Yes,' said Elsie. 'Try not to knock more bags over.'

'I won't,' said Sylphine, sounding hurt.

'Anyone would think I was clumsy.'

'All I have to do now is get rid of this.' Elsie walked to the mirror and pulled at the draped sheet. It slithered down in a cloud of dust. The mirror beneath was coated with a thick layer of grime.

'I'll carry it down,' offered Joey. 'Where shall I put it?'

'Out by the privy for the Howlers to pinch. Wait, I'll just give it a quick rub. It's filthy.'

She took a duster from her apron pocket, vigorously rubbed at the glass – then jumped back with a surprised squeal!

Someone was glaring out at her!

The figure was short, plump and green. Not the green of sweet little frogs or freshly mown lawns. His skin was the colour of a scummy pond. He had a big nose, large ears and a downturned mouth that looked like he'd been sucking on lemons. He was completely bald, except for a small tuft of green hair that sprang upright on the top of his head, like a stand of tiny trees on a hill.

Strangely, he was wearing rumpled grey pyjamas with faded green stripes that had clearly been washed once too often. The middle button was missing on the pyjama top, showing an expanse of green tummy. On his feet were hairy brown slippers.

He glowered at Elsie and snapped, '*What?*'

'Oh!' said Elsie. 'You must be the genie? I didn't know you were

still in there.'

'Of course I'm the flaming genie. Daft question. I was *asleep*. You know? When you close your eyes and don't want to be disturbed?'

'If you're a genie, where's your curly moustache and smiling, helpful manner?' asked Joey.

'That's lamp genies. I'm a mirror genie. We don't bother with all that poncey stuff.'

'So mirror genies wear old pyjamas and granddad slippers, do they?'

'They do when they've just been got out of bed, pal.' The genie's eyes flickered around. 'Where's *she* gone? Madame Snooty?'

'If you mean Witch Sharp, she's out visiting a friend,' said Elsie, Customer Service Rule One clicking in: Be Friendly, even to rude people. 'Do you have a name, Mr . . . ?'

'Frank,' snapped the genie. 'Frank by name,

frank by nature. I tell it like it is.'

'Do you give out three wishes?' asked Sylphine excitedly. 'Because my hair gets these awful split ends and I've always wanted a pet unicorn—'

'What did I just say, cloth ears? I'm a *mirror* genie. We don't do wishes.'

"I thought all genies could give out wishes," said Joey.

"I didn't say I couldn't. I said I don't."

'What do you do, then?' asked Joey. 'Apart from be mean?'

'I tell the truth, son. You know. *Mirror, mirror on the wall, who is the fairest of us all*? Not you. That kind of thing.'

'Sounds mean to me,' said Sylphine.

'True, though,' said Frank. 'Especially in your case. Take those dead flowers out of your hair. They look stupid.'

Sylphine's lower lip wobbled.

'Leave her alone,' said Joey. 'She's sensitive.'

'Well, she shouldn't go round with a head like an overgrown allotment.'

'Frank,' said Elsie, now feeling quite cross. Customer Service only took you so far. Sometimes, you had to draw the line. 'You like the truth, so I'm going to be honest with you. We're moving you out. It's time you found a new home.'

'What you talkin' about?' said Frank.

'You can't stay here any more. But I'm sure the Howler Sisters will love you.'

'What?'

'She means you're surplus to requirements,' said Joey. 'Sorry, mate.' He stepped forward, picked up the mirror and tucked it under his arm.

'Oi!' shouted Frank, as his reflection turned on its side. 'You put me down right now!'

'I'll help,' said Sylphine. Arms outstretched, she moved forward – and the inevitable happened. She tripped over the piled rubbish bags. Arms whirling, she lurched forward and fell into Joey. The mirror slipped from beneath his arm—

CRRRAAASH!

It landed on the floor and smashed into a thousand pieces. Elsie covered her eyes to protect them from flying glass. When she dared to look again, much to her dismay, there stood Frank – a reflection no more. No, now Frank was very much here in the flesh, standing in his slippers in a pile of broken glass.

'Hey,' he said, a grin on his face. 'Free at last!'

And with a pop, he vanished.

'Sorry, Elsie,' said Sylphine, picking shards of glass from her moccasins. 'I just tripped.'

'It's okay,' said Elsie. 'Accidents happen. At least we've got rid of Frank.'

'He was horrible,' said Sylphine. 'I never want to see him again!'

'Well, tough potatoes, because here I am,' sneered a voice from behind.

And there was Frank, leaning against the door. 'You don't

get rid of me that easily. You're clumsy, you are. Like a cross-eyed goose with its foot in a plaster cast.'

With that, he vanished again.

This was the first of many such appearances. Elsie was wrong. They hadn't got rid of him at all. Instead, they'd just set him free to sneak up on them and be mean.

'You're too puny for a post boy,' said Frank, materializing on the path as Joey set off on his round. 'What happens to your poor wittle arms when dey make you carry dose *gweat* big heavy parcels? Does oo *dwop* dem?'

Back in the tower, Corbett nearly fell off his perch when Frank shot out of the hole in the sink and stood sneering on the draining board.

'You're a right pain, aren't you?' Frank said to him. 'Think you're so wise and clever, but you're birdbrained. Do us all a favour and fly away, pal. And do something about those bald bits, it's not a good look.'

'I don't like you,' said Frank to Elsie, giving her a shock by showing up in the larder. 'You're just a silly shop girl who thinks you're special because you can do a couple of baby spells.'

'Pink looks awful on you,' said Frank to Sylphine, just as she was about to enter her cottage.

'Take my advice, rethink your wardrobe. Face it, you're never going to look like a wood sprite.'

'You're a stray, right?' said Frank to Nuisance, who was curled up on the step with one eye open, hoping that Elsie would bring his breakfast soon. 'Nobody wants you because you're scruffy and smell like an old carpet.'

In fact, in just a few hours Frank managed to insult and offend *everybody*! What were they going to do?

Chapter Five
ANOTHER BUSY NIGHT

Magenta arrived back at dusk. The front door crashed open and she fell in, almost dropping the large cardboard box she was carrying.

'Here she comes,' muttered Corbett from his sick perch. 'In a mood, by the looks of it.'

'That dog is such a nuisance!' snapped Magenta. 'Always lying in the way.'

She dumped the box on the table, kicked off her shoes and sank into the rocking chair.

'That reminds me,' said Elsie. 'I haven't given

him his supper.' She felt guilty. Accidentally setting Frank loose was very much on her mind – so much so that she had completely forgotten Nuisance's evening sausage. Neither had she ruffled his head, pulled the burrs from his coat or taken him for a walk today.

She went to the door and looked out. The doorstep was empty. The trees were still and quiet. The owls were out.

'Nuisance?' she shouted. 'Where are you?'

Silence.

Elsie went back inside. 'I'll give him a minute. Did you get everything?'

'I did,' said Magenta. 'But that's the last time I'm going to Wendy's. First off, she had me counting frogs in a bucket. Said they were too quick for her. Then she got me watering her herbs, which grow on a hill that's too steep for her. Then I spent hours helping her find her missing wand, which she'd forgotten was propping open a window. I had raw shredded cabbage with grated onions for lunch while she lurked in the pantry eating sausages.'

Outside, a bush rustled. Roused by the word sausages and Elsie's earlier call, Nuisance emerged, trotted back to the doorstep and hopefully scratched at the door. But inside, nobody heard. They were too busy discussing Wendy Snipe.

Nuisance gave a little sigh and lay down. Forgotten again. What was life coming to?

'She must be wise,' said Elsie. 'Getting you to do all that for her.'

'Oh, yes,' said Magenta. 'Wendy knows all the tricks. And the entire time, she never, ever stops talking. I am utterly exhausted.

What's for supper?'

'Carrot soup,' said Elsie. 'Freshly made. And I'll make us some toast.'

'Good.' Magenta glared at Corbett. 'I see you're still drooping about like you've been attacked by a lawnmower.'

'Nice to see you too,' said Corbett sulkily. 'Sad to hear you've had a horrible day. Oh, my mistake, I mean glad.'

Over supper, Elsie told Magenta all about Frank's escape.

'So the genie's out.' Magenta took a bite of toast. 'That's annoying.'

'Disaster, more like,' croaked Corbett. Glumly, he took a sip of the lemon and honey drink Elsie had made for his sore throat.

'He's insufferable.'

'No worse than you, surely?' said Magenta.

'He is,' said Elsie quickly, to divert an argument. 'He's much, much meaner than Corbett. And he hasn't even got the excuse of moulting.'

'See?' said Corbett with a sniff. 'Some people care.'

'Can't we get rid of Frank?' asked Elsie.

'I doubt it.' Magenta shook her head. 'He came with the tower, you see. When you move into a tower like this, you have to take on all the old rubbish that comes with it. Miserable moulting ravens—'

'Oi!' protested Corbett.

'Genie-haunted mirrors,' went on Magenta. 'Funny stains. Weird rumbles. In return, you get all the special features. Lots of cake. No need to cook or clean. Regular change of scenery. All part of the package.'

'*What the Tower doth have, the Tower doth keep,*' quoted Corbett from his perch, adding, 'And who are you calling miserable?'

'But you suggested putting the mirror out for the Howlers to take,' Elsie pointed out.

'I assumed Frank had already left of his own accord. I didn't know he was sleeping.' Magenta gave a sigh. 'No, I'm afraid the only way to get rid of him is to use a clever trick or riddle to get him back into another mirror. But all the genies are wise to that now, it's been done too often. So we'll just have to hope he keeps out of the way.' Elsie looked over at the box of ingredients. 'Did you get everything from Wendy?'

'Yes, eventually.'

'Good. So we can start making up the spells.'

'What? Now?' Magenta put down her spoon and frowned.

'No time to lose,' said Elsie. 'They have to go off tomorrow.'

'Don't expect me to help,' said Corbett. 'I'm not up to it.' He gave a pitiful little cough.

'I wouldn't want you to,' said Magenta. 'Sneezing and wheezing and shedding everywhere. You're a health hazard.'

'That does it,' said Corbett. 'Farewell for ever. Probably.' And he flew out of the window into the night. A single black feather floated down and landed in Magenta's empty soup bowl.

'Well, I can't do it all myself,' said Magenta. 'I need assistance, so I'll have to leave it until he comes round—'

'I'll help,' said Elsie.

'You were up all last night tidying the office.

Aren't you tired?'

'I'm fine,' said Elsie. 'I had a nap earlier.'

She had, too. A little afternoon snooze that had really done the trick. It happened in the lovely blue bedroom that she thought of as her own here at the tower. The room was just the same as it had been last time, with the picture of Pickles' Emporium still on the wall, but now showing the shop looking smart in its new coat of paint.

Ten minutes after closing her eyes, she had woken up feeling refreshed and ready for anything. There was something about that bed.

'Oh,' said Magenta. 'Well, in that case, I suppose . . .'

'I'll clear the table and we'll get started.'

'Mmm,' said Magenta. She didn't sound keen.

Elsie blew up the fire with bellows to heat the cauldron while Magenta unpacked the cardboard box.

'Done?' called Magenta. 'Now shut the window, draw the curtain and turn down the lamps. Magic is all about atmosphere. Get out the pestle and mortar and the scales. You'll be doing a lot of grinding and weighing. And look in the bottom cupboard. There's a box full of empty bottles and jars and whatnot. Quick, quick, we don't want to be all night.'

As soon as the flames were crackling, Elsie moved to the table and examined the labels on the various boxes, packets, tins, tubs and bottles that crowded the table. They looked like the sort of ingredients you would use to bake a cake – except for the names.

'"Old Man's Stubble",' read Elsie. '"Scabious

Foxbane. Mother Sibyl's Syrup. Wizard's Honkweed. Faraway Seeds. Desiccated Moon Root. Elf Raising Flour." Will we be using all of these?'

'Yes. There are one or two rhymes you'll need to learn as well. And a few dance steps.'

'*Dance steps?*'

'Some recipes call for the odd bit of hopping about. You'll have to do it, my feet are killing me.' Magenta sat heavily in the rocking chair and stretched out her long, bony, red-stockinged feet. 'Go and deal with the Howlers, then we'll start.'

'What do you mean, deal with the How—'

Right on cue, there came a warning bark from the front step, followed by a growl.

'Ah,' said Elsie. 'Right.' And she went to the door to deal with the Howlers.

Nuisance was up on his feet, fur bristling and teeth bared. He didn't like the Howler Sisters.

They stood in moonlight, a safe distance from the teeth and the slavering jaws. Evie and Ada. Two sweet little old ladies in pastel dresses, with matching parasols. Tight grey curls, winning smiles – and long, furry tails protruding from slits in the back of their gowns!

'Elsie!' cried Evie. 'How lovely to see you again!'

'Good evening, ladies,' said Elsie. 'Shush, Nuisance, I don't need your help.'

'We heard you were back, dear,' said Ada. 'We thought we'd pay a little call.'

'I'm afraid it's not a good time,' said Elsie.

'Yes, we noticed the drawn curtains and the smoking chimney. Is Magenta there?'

'She's . . . resting.'

'Oh, that's a shame,' said Evie. 'Because I'm sad to say we've got a complaint. About the genie.'

'Oh, dear,' said Elsie. 'I'm afraid he got out by accident. Has he been bothering you?'

'Oh, yes!' cried the Howlers in chorus.

'He's so *rude!*' said Ada, 'Isn't he, Evie? What he said about a certain aspect of our anatomy!

Of which we are rightly proud!'

Their tails swished angrily.

'And he as good as called us thieves!' said Evie. 'Us!'

'Leaping out with his insults and those *dreadful* pyjamas,' said Ada. 'Something must be done.'

'I'm really sorry,' said Elsie. 'We'll see what we can do. But right now, we're in the middle of . . . cooking.'

Gently but firmly, she closed the door. Nuisance stood growling until the Howlers vanished into the trees, then lay down, buried his nose under his paws and, in the absence of any supper, went to sleep.

'Gone?' enquired Magenta as Elsie returned to the kitchen.

'Gone,' said Elsie. 'Complaining about Frank.

He's popping up being truthful and they don't like it.'

'Tough. Frank's a problem for another day.' Magenta sat back in the rocking chair and closed her eyes. 'Right. To work. We'll start with Belt Up Balm. Weigh out eight ounces of Wizard's Honkweed, throw two pinches over your shoulder, hop on your left foot for the count of seven, put the rest of it in the mortar and start grinding.'

It was a long, long night. Magenta's definition of work was to slump in the chair and order Elsie about.

Elsie ground, weighed, measured, poured, chopped, whisked and ground some more. She made tea. She stirred the cauldron, and learned a little rhyme for the Last Word Lozenges, to be chanted whilst rolling dough into balls.

It went:

Brain quick, tongue slick,
Let the lozenge do the trick.

There was another rhyme that went with the Pep-Up Powder, to be performed seven times while grinding the mixture in the mortar. That one went:

Pep-Up Powder can't be beat.
Puts the pop into your feet.

The chanting was fun, but the dancing was a bit embarrassing. Elsie felt silly, prancing about on her own. But she did it. With magic, there is no cutting of corners.

Once all the various pills and potions were made, they had to be decanted into the right containers. Labels had to be stuck on. Everything needed to be packed into boxes, and names and addresses added. And then, of

course, there was the washing-up.

But Elsie was enjoying herself. She kept going, while Magenta sighed and yawned and demanded more tea.

As dawn crept over the forest, Elsie finished rinsing out the cauldron.

'Done!' she announced. A gentle snore came from the armchair. Elsie walked over and gave Magenta a little shake.

'Huh? What?' Magenta looked up blearily.

'All finished. Everything's packed and ready to go, except for Mr Eric Smalldon's back rub.'

Elsie was concerned about this. Mr Eric Smalldon was the only

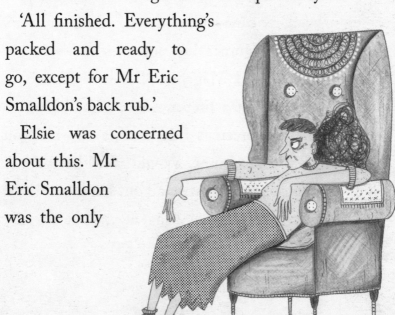

one of Magenta's long-term customers who seemed to be largely happy with her service. Elsie had found several letters from him saying how delighted he was with Sharp's Hot Back Rub. He was the kind of repeat customer that Sharp Spells needed, so he of all people deserved to get a new supply as soon as possible.

'It's just chilly-chilli oil,' said Magenta. 'Hot and cold at the same time.' She frowned. 'Botheration. I'm sure I asked Wendy for a jar.'

'Well, we can't let him down,' said Elsie. 'He's your best customer. Just pop back and—'

'Never!' said Magenta. 'I've had enough of Wendy to last a lifetime. No, I shall have to go to the Sorcerer's Bazaar after all. Tell you what, you can come. Would you like that? A little shopping trip after all our hard work?'

Elsie reflected that Magenta hadn't actually

done much of the work. But she was too polite to say so, and a trip to a real magic shop wasn't something to be missed.

'Yes, please!' she said. 'Maybe I'll pick up some tips to improve the Emporium.'

'Possibly. We can take the tower. It likes a change of scene from time to time. We leave after breakfast.'

Chapter Six
THE STAR ROOM

The following morning, Elsie and Magenta and Corbett were in the kitchen eating a strange but enjoyable breakfast of toast, apples, pancakes and coconut cake. Elsie couldn't eat as much as usual. She was too excited about the prospect of the trip. The tower's biggest secret was about to be revealed.

Corbett had flown in through the open window as soon as Elsie had laid out the food and was now pecking up crumbs with relish. His night away from Magenta had clearly done him good. His appetite was back and there was a hint of new plumage around his neck.

'I bet she made you do everything. Sat in the chair and issued her orders, right?' he said, nodding at the boxes and packages piled by the door.

'So what if I did?' said Magenta. 'Do it yourself, that's the way to learn.' She set down her teacup and stood up. 'Ready, Elsie? I'll show you the Wheel.'

'Oh-ho!' cried Corbett. 'We're taking a trip? *Now* you're talking!'

'Wheel?' said Elsie, hastily swallowing the last of her toast. 'What Wheel?'

'The Wheel in the Star Room,' said Magenta.

'Star Room?'

'It's in the basement.'

'There's a basement? You didn't say anything

about wheels or star rooms or basements when you showed me round the first time,' said Elsie to Corbett.

'She said not to,' said Corbett, nodding at Magenta. 'Blame her.'

'Everything in its own good time,' said the witch. 'The tower doesn't reveal its secrets to everyone. You have to earn its trust. Tower! Access to the Star Room, if you please.'

There was a faint vibration in the walls and suddenly the rug on the kitchen floor gave a little jerk. Ripples spread across its surface. Then, smoothly and efficiently, it rolled itself back, exposing a large, grey flagstone that looked identical to all the other flagstones making up the kitchen floor. Until . . .

The stone levitated! Up it rose, slowly and steadily, revealing a square hole in the floor,

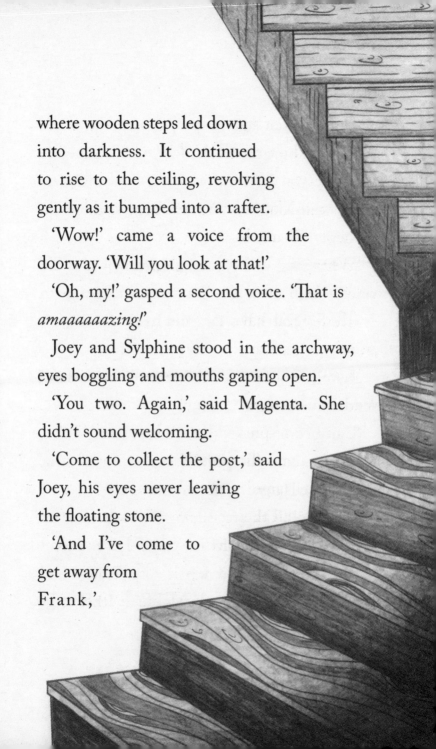

where wooden steps led down into darkness. It continued to rise to the ceiling, revolving gently as it bumped into a rafter.

'Wow!' came a voice from the doorway. 'Will you look at that!'

'Oh, my!' gasped a second voice. 'That is *amaaaaaazing!*'

Joey and Sylphine stood in the archway, eyes boggling and mouths gaping open.

'You two. Again,' said Magenta. She didn't sound welcoming.

'Come to collect the post,' said Joey, his eyes never leaving the floating stone.

'And I've come to get away from Frank,'

said Sylphine. 'He keeps popping up at my house and being hateful.'

'Well, you've come at a very inconvenient time,' said Magenta. 'We're about to move the tower.'

'Where to?' asked Joey, staring down at the dark hole in the floor. 'Somewhere exciting?'

'The Sorcerer's Bazaar,' said Elsie. 'It's a magic shop.'

'Excellent!' crowed Corbett. 'I'll get some feather restorer!'

'Can I come?' asked Joey. 'I can, can't I?'

'What about the post?' Elsie reminded him. 'Those spells need to go out today.'

'They will, the second we get back. That's a promise. Oh, please let me come. Let me come let me come let me come—'

'And me!' interrupted Sylphine. 'I never go

anywhere. Oh, please!'

'Let me come let me come let me . . .'

'This is Elsie's first trip,' said Magenta. 'She's taking the Wheel. She might not want you tagging along. I wouldn't. I find both of you highly irritating. But it's up to her.'

'Of course they must come,' said Elsie loyally. She was rewarded with a whoop from Joey and a hug from Sylphine.

'What's the Bazaar like?' asked Sylphine excitedly. 'I bet it's wonderful.'

'There's a lot of cheap rubbish to wade through before you get to the better stuff,' said Magenta. 'People think if they put "mystic" in front, it'll sell. Mystic chalk. Mystic bathplugs. Mystic forks. Mystic – I don't know.'

'Mystic sticks,' supplied Corbett. 'Dipped in treacle, so they're mystic sticky sticks.'

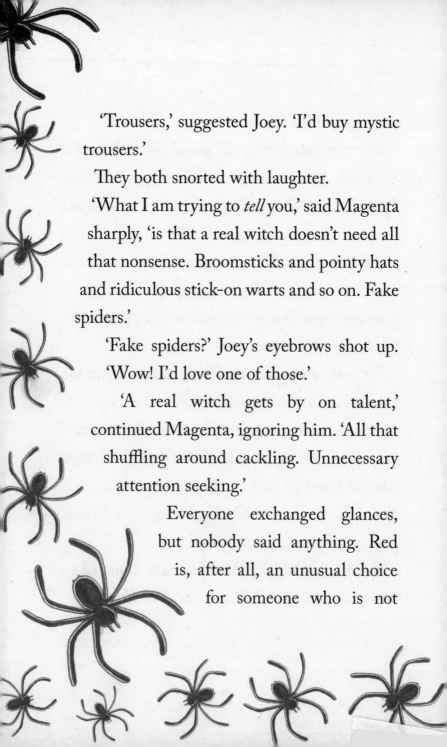

'Trousers,' suggested Joey. 'I'd buy mystic trousers.'

They both snorted with laughter.

'What I am trying to *tell* you,' said Magenta sharply, 'is that a real witch doesn't need all that nonsense. Broomsticks and pointy hats and ridiculous stick-on warts and so on. Fake spiders.'

'Fake spiders?' Joey's eyebrows shot up. 'Wow! I'd love one of those.'

'A real witch gets by on talent,' continued Magenta, ignoring him. 'All that shuffling around cackling. Unnecessary attention seeking.'

Everyone exchanged glances, but nobody said anything. Red is, after all, an unusual choice for someone who is not seeking attention.

'Do they sell gowns for wood sprites?' asked Sylphine. 'And scarves? I love scarves. Long, floaty ones. I dance with them in the moonlight. Are there scarves?'

'I'm buying a fake spider,' announced Joey. 'Or I would, if I had any money.'

'Magenta will pay,' said Corbett cheerfully. 'She's got an account there.'

'By all means,' said Magenta, sounding quite gracious for once. 'Let nobody call me a cheapskate. You may purchase one moderately priced item each, for which I will pay. Enough talk, let's go.'

Magenta started off down the dark steps. Elsie followed, with Corbett on her shoulder. Next came Sylphine, tripping over her dress, and Joey brought up the rear. At the bottom, they stood in the dim pool of light filtering down from the kitchen. Ahead stretched a low, dark passageway.

'Lights, Tower, if you please!' commanded Magenta.

Instantly, tiny dots of light began appearing like fireflies, lining the passage walls.

'Come on,' said Magenta, and strode off. Everyone fell in line behind.

The tunnel twisted and turned, the tiny lights proving the only illumination. This went on for some time. One thing was certain. The basement was surprisingly *big*.

Finally, Magenta came to a halt.

'Here we are,' she announced. 'There's a curtain ahead.'

There was a swishing noise . . .

And Elsie saw . . .

Stars!

They were everywhere. Above and all around
– thousands of them, dazzling and dizzying,
speckling the walls and ceiling – if indeed there
were walls or a ceiling. In fact, it didn't look
like a room. It looked like a sparkling night sky
stretching in every direction. The floor seemed
to consist of shimmering white sand, from
which rose ghostly tendrils of silver mist.

Most amazing of all was the Wheel. It
hovered in the centre at around waist height.
It had eight spokes, just like a ship's wheel, and
it glowed with a pure white light. Little blue
sparkles twinkled over the spokes as it slowly
revolved in mid-air.

'Oh,' breathed Elsie. She didn't know what

she had expected, but it wasn't this.

'It's so pretty!' gasped Sylphine.

Joey just let out an awestruck whistle.

'So,' said Elsie. 'What do I do?'

'Approach the Wheel,' said Magenta. 'Take hold of the two topmost spokes, state the required destination slowly and clearly, remembering to say please. Give it one full rotation. That's it.'

'Come on,' said Corbett from Elsie's shoulder. 'Trust me, it doesn't hurt.'

Chapter Seven
THE SORCERER'S BAZAAR

The floor felt strange. Spongy.

Like walking on clouds, thought Elsie.

Silvery mist swirled around her ankles as she moved forward. All around, the stars whirled. As she approached the Wheel, it slowed to a standstill, as though it was waiting for her. Cautiously, Elsie reached out and grasped two of the spokes. There was a cool, tingling sensation in her palms that felt a little like mild pins and needles. It wasn't unpleasant.

'Words next,' urged Corbett into her ear.

'Tower,' said Elsie, 'can you take us to the Sorcerer's Bazaar, please?'

The stars froze in their tracks. There was a strange, see-sawing sensation in Elsie's stomach, and the pins and needles in her palms suddenly intensified. The Wheel began to turn slowly and the spokes she was holding moved round and out of her grasp, to be replaced by the next two. There came the sound of faraway tinkling bells . . . and the overpowering smell of roses . . . and the floor seemed to fall away . . . and then there came a dazzling explosion of white light that made everyone screw their eyes shut . . . and then . . .

'That's more than enough, thank you, Tower,' Magenta said. 'No need to overdo it. I'd lose the smell, it's a step too far. You can all open your eyes, we've arrived.'

Elsie opened her eyes. Gone were the whirling stars and the silvery mist. Instead she found that they were standing in a small basement room. Where there had been the ship's wheel, she now held an old wooden cart wheel. Ancient bits of cobwebby equipment leaned against the walls – a broken deckchair, a rusty lawnmower, a wheelbarrow with both handles missing.

'It likes to put on a show,' explained Corbett. 'One of its party pieces, that. Just an illusion, but effective, especially the first time. After that, between you and me, it gets a bit samey. You can put that cartwheel down now, Elsie. Let's go shopping!'

The first thing Elsie saw when they opened the

front door of the tower was the back view of Nuisance. He was sitting bolt upright on the doorstep, ears erect and fur on end. A surprised growl was coming from deep within his throat.

'It's all right,' said Elsie, crouching down and patting his head. She felt really guilty. In the excitement of being allowed to move the tower she had forgotten all about him again, out there on the doorstep waiting in vain for breakfast and then finding the tower move without warning. 'Gave you a shock, did it?' Her eyes took in what rose before them. 'Oh, my! No wonder.'

No longer were they in the middle of the sunny forest. Instead, rising directly before them, silhouetted against a dark blue sky, was a vast, white, domed building. A sweeping flight of wide steps led up to huge, glittering black glass doors with tall pillars on either side.

Above the doors was a blazing sign picked out in golden, illuminated letters.

'Right,' said Magenta briskly. 'Let's get this over with.' She stepped over Nuisance and strode towards the flight of steps. The rest of them followed as behind them the tower slowly buried itself in a bank of thick fog.

When Magenta reached the top of the stairs she rapped the glass with her red-gloved hand. 'Open up,' she ordered. 'Witch Magenta Sharp demanding entrance.'

From out of the air, there came a strange, unexpected crackling. And then—

'Valued customers!' boomed a rich, plummy voice. 'Welcome to the Sorcerer's Bazaar! Here begins the ultimate shopping experience! All your magical requirements under one roof! Marketplace on the ground floor. Hall of

THE
SORCERER'S BAZAAR

Mirrors and Menagerie of Fearsome Creatures and Exotic Beasts on the first. Fortune Teller, Bookshop and Reasonably Priced Café on the second. Loose Magical Ingredients and Specialist Spells on the third. And why not add an extra thrill to your day by trying out the last word in modern inter-floor transport, the Lift, operated by a fully-trained attendant who will ensure a swift, smooth journey. For your convenience, we have a pay at the end policy. Select your purchases, place in the baskets provided, spend hugely and finally make your way to the tills. Shoplifters are always prosecuted. Damaged goods must be paid for. Save time by having the correct change. Happy shopping!'

There came a short fanfare of trumpets, and the black doors drew smoothly aside. Magenta marched in with Joey and Sylphine hot on her heels. Corbett took off from Elsie's shoulder and followed them.

Nuisance lay down and put his head on his paws.

'Not coming?' asked Elsie. 'All right, I understand. You're not an indoor dog. You'll wait here for us, yes?'

'Come on, Elsie!' called Corbett impatiently. 'There's a lot to see.'

Elsie ran through the doors.

Nuisance gave a little sigh. A few minutes ago he had been sitting on the doorstep thinking about sausages, when all of a sudden the world wobbled and he went transparent! He could actually see the crack on the step through his paws! It hadn't lasted more than a split second, but still. And then everything changed and they were somewhere else entirely. Somewhere glittery that smelled funny. Elsie was here, and that made things a little better, but now he was on his own again, and still hungry. It was all most unsettling. He looked sadly at the doors Elsie had gone through – perhaps it wouldn't be long before she was back and gave him a lovely tasty sausage. He would just have to be patient.

But as Elsie joined the others who were waiting for her inside, she didn't give Nuisance another thought because before her was a whole new world! And it was incredible!

It was the noise that hit first. The sound of hundreds of happy shoppers going about their business combined with stallholders yelling their wares, plus regular bangs, explosions and fizzing eruptions of little green sparks as various spells were demonstrated. The heaving market hall was jam-packed with stalls selling – well, by the looks of it – every magical item ever invented. Wands, broomsticks, seven-league boots, pointy hats, cauldrons, crystal balls, lucky charms, flying carpets, capes of darkness, cloaks of invisibility, wishing rings . . . The booming voice at the entrance had been right. You could get *anything* here. A wide, sweeping staircase led up to the mysterious higher floors.

Customers weaved between the stalls, poking and prodding and examining the merchandise. Not at all the sort of customers that Elsie was used to in the Emporium. Wizardly beards, pointy hats, robes emblazoned with stars and moons and pointed elvish ears were not at all the sort of thing you tended to see in Smallbridge, which was the kind of place where people nudged and whispered if anyone had the nerve to wear a slightly unconventional hat.

'So what do you think?' asked Corbett, flying onto her shoulder. 'In your professional opinion. A good shop, or what?'

'Well, it's certainly . . . different,' said Elsie. She was staring at a group of squat, sulky-looking goblins in flat caps, who were staging a sit-down protest because they had come a day too late and missed out on the one-for-the-price-of-two offer. You could tell they were goblins, because they wore matching T-shirts saying so. People were just stepping over them.

Elsie's eyes didn't know where to go next there was so much activity and movement.

Even more fascinating was the fact that most customers were closely followed by floating wire baskets. Some were empty but most were piled high with purchases.

Creatures and Exotic Beasts

Hall of Mirrors

Café

Fortune Teller

Bookshop

Loose Magical Ingredients
And Specialist Spells

LIFT

Wish Rings

Wand

Floating baskets, Elsie thought. *What a clever idea. Imagine if we had those in the Emporium. Would that bring the customers in, I wonder?*

'It would frighten them off,' said Magenta, reading her mind. 'Smallbridge isn't ready for a shop like this. Although, as I say, there's an awful lot of rubbish here too.'

'Exciting rubbish, though,' said Joey, finally finding his voice. Both he and Sylphine had been standing stock-still, struck speechless by the wonder of it all. 'Fantastic, amazing, tremendously wonderful rubbish. Right, Aggie?'

'Did you hear what that voice said?' said Sylphine in a strangled voice. She was clearly finding it hard to breathe. 'Exotic beasts! Do you think . . . Oh, could it be they'll have a *unicorn?*'

A pile of wire baskets stood just inside the

door. The top five detached themselves, floated down and hovered alongside each of the group at waist height. Corbett's basket shrank to a tiny bird size and hovered just above Elsie's shoulder.

'Get off,' said Magenta, waving hers away. 'I don't need you. I only want one item.'

'I could do with one of these on my post round!' cried Joey, poking at the basket by his side. To his delight, it gave him a friendly little nudge in return.

'Right. Follow me, everyone,' said Magenta. 'I would like us to stay together. It's easy to get separate—'

'Yoo-hoo! Madge! Magenta!'

A beaming little woman with corrugated grey curls was making her way towards them, wielding a large black handbag that she was using as a sort of snowplough to carve a path

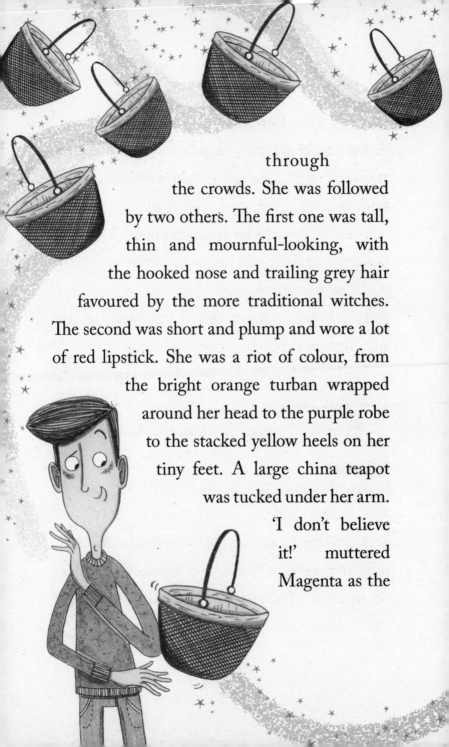

through
the crowds. She was followed
by two others. The first one was tall,
thin and mournful-looking, with
the hooked nose and trailing grey hair
favoured by the more traditional witches.
The second was short and plump and wore a lot
of red lipstick. She was a riot of colour, from
the bright orange turban wrapped
around her head to the purple robe
to the stacked yellow heels on her
tiny feet. A large china teapot
was tucked under her arm.

'I don't believe
it!' muttered
Magenta as the

three of them bore down. 'It's Wendy.'

'Fancy seeing you, Madge!' cried the little beaming one. 'You never said you was coming here today!'

'I don't *want* to be here,' snapped Magenta. 'I'm here because you forgot to put in the chilly-chilli oil yesterday.'

'Did I? Sorry about that. I just bumped into Maureen and Shirley, look!'

'Hello, Magenta,' sighed Maureen, the mournful one.

'I knew it!' said Shirley, the one holding the teapot. 'Knew she'd be here today. Saw it in the tea leaves. *You will meet an old friend*, they said.'

'Ain't this lovely?' went on Wendy. 'All here together at the same time!' She beamed at Elsie. 'Is this her? The girl you was telling me about yesterday? The promising one you're training up?'

Magenta gave a sigh. 'Elsie, meet Wendy the Wise Woman of Clackham Common. And Maureen the Hag of Heaving Heath. And Madame Shirley, Fortune Teller to the Stars.'

'Tea leaves a speciality,' added Madame Shirley, nodding at the teapot. 'Cross my palm with gold and all will be revealed.'

'I thought it was silver,' said Maureen.

'I've put my fees up,' said Shirley. 'Inflation.'

'I don't charge for my wisdom,' Wendy informed them. 'People just give me stuff. I make more that way because they don't want to appear tight. Pleased to meet you, Elsie, dear.'

'How do you do?' said Elsie politely.

Training me up? she thought. *Promising? She*

thinks I'm promising.

Magenta didn't hand out praise easily. Elsie couldn't help feeling pleased.

'Dunno about anyone else, but I'm ready for a cuppa,' said Wendy. 'You can catch us up on your news, Madge. I didn't get time to ask yesterday. Too busy talking about meself, ha, ha!' She gave Elsie a nudge. 'They'll tell you. Never stop talking, me. Unusual for a wise woman. We're normally good listeners.'

'I heard you're having trouble with the mail order,' said Maureen to Magenta.

'Magic Board on the case, *I* heard,' said Shirley. 'Threatening to take away your licence.'

'Shame,' all three chorused together, sounding sorrowful but quite pleased at the same time.

'I can't imagine where you got that from,' replied Magenta. 'Business is booming. That's why I need an apprentice. This is a flying visit. I have a lot of stuff needs posting today. The post boy needs to get back. He just came along for the ride. So did the other girl.'

'What post boy?' asked Shirley, staring at the space where Joey wasn't.

'What other girl? asked Maureen. Sylphine was also missing.

'They've gone off after spiders and unicorns,' said Corbett from Elsie's shoulder. 'Bored with all this endless yakking.'

'Still got it, then,' observed Maureen. 'The miserable crow. Or is it a rook? Or just a very dirty parrot?'

'Raven,' said Corbett spiritedly. 'May pea-brained pigeons spit on your ignorance.' Which was a rude reply, but at least it showed he was beginning to feel better.

'Well, we really must get on,' went on Magenta. 'I'm just here to get the chilly-chilli oil and give Elsie a quick tour of the sort of stuff that's available—'

'Ah, she'll be all right looking around on 'er own.' Wendy beamed at Elsie. 'You'll be all right, won't you, ducks? Take your time, Madge'll find you in a bit.'

'Look, I really can't—' began Magenta.

'You're coming and that's that,' said Wendy, linking her arm with Magenta's. 'How often do we all get together for a chinwag?'

'So shall we go?' asked Shirley.

'Yep,' said Maureen and Wendy.

And with that, the four of them disappeared.

'How do they *do* that?' said Elsie. 'Just – vanish? I wish Magenta would teach me.'

'It's a witch thing,' said Corbett. 'I'm going to take a quick flyover, try and find some feather restorer. Back in two shakes!'

And with that, he was gone, the dinky bird-sized basket whizzing along behind.

Elsie was left on her own. That was no bad thing. She was in a strange shop on the other side of the counter and free to go exploring. That didn't happen often.

Right, she thought. *Here I go. This is going to be fun!*

'Wrong again, shop girl,' said a sneering voice from behind. 'Shouldn't you be serving?'

It was Frank.

Chapter Eight
MEANWHILE...

I'm in a Magic Shop! thought Joey as he moved between the stalls. *Brilliant! This is as good as the day I became a post boy and got the Sack.*

Joey liked being a post boy. The hours were flexible and his mum was so proud of him that she'd cried at the ceremony when he got the special Sack.

Joey liked the hat and the badge. He liked walking and whistling cheerily. He liked being alone in his head, making up jokes and pretending there were bears behind trees. He liked people too.

The only drawback was that most days it was a very ordinary job, delivering bills, cards and letters with the occasional chat and cup of tea. Things only hotted up when witches' exploding parcels and magical towers were involved. So, even though he wouldn't give up his job for anything, right now he had been transported to a world of dazzling new opportunities and was determined to enjoy every last second.

One item, he thought. *I can choose just one item to take back home.*

But how? How was he supposed pick just one thing? There was so much stuff – and it was all great! Every stall held its own delights, all of which he wanted. He wanted the lucky tin horseshoe badges and the fire-damaged candles. He wanted the swishy purple cape with star signs and the false wizard whiskers. He was spellbound by the genie outfit stall. A green satin turban with a huge red jewel in the middle was particularly eye-catching.

He wanted the portable camping cauldron that could fold into an emergency stool. He wanted the cheap in-hand spells that exploded like fireworks, letting off horrible smells. He wanted the fake wiggly worms and the rubber snakes that hissed and the cushion that made a rude noise when you sat on it. He wanted the wand that played music, even though the tune was horrible and stopped working halfway through the first wave. He wanted one of the small, eager, chained-up flying carpets. He wanted a flat cap, the sort worn by goblins. He wanted everything.

The stallholders wanted him to have everything too.

'Fancy one of those, do we, sir?'

'Try it on, sir. Ooh, you do look handsome.'

'You so suit a turban, love. Green's your colour. Matches your eyes.'

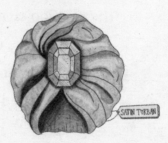

'Word of advice, son, next time it catches fire,

let it go. Burned your thumb? We don't accept responsibility, says on the packet. But, tell you what, I'll do you six for the price of seven, how's that?'

There was just so much to look at! Joey tried on a Cloak of Invisibility. It was made of some weird, shiny material that engulfed him from head to toe, like a wearable tent. He asked the stallholder – a teenage gnome with pimples – for a mirror so that he could see the effect. The gnome didn't have one.

'So how do I know it's working?' asked Joey.

'Well, *I* can't see you,' said the gnome.

'Yes, but you would say that, wouldn't you? Because you want me to buy it.'

'Why wouldn't you buy it? Unique, innit?'

'How come you've got so many for sale, then?'

'I dunno, I'm minding the stall for my uncle. Do you want it or not?'

But Joey couldn't decide what to choose, there was just too much . . .

He was getting distracted by his wire basket too. It bobbed perkily behind him, maintaining just the right distance – friendly, reachable, but not crowding him. When Joey stopped, the basket stopped. When he moved, the basket moved.

He was just passing a stall selling spinning wheels when he felt the basket bump him playfully on the bum. Joey turned round.

The basket gave a jolly little mid-air bounce, radiating a sort of puppy-like eagerness.

'What?' said Joey. 'You want to play? Is that it?'

He found a quieter space behind one of the duller stalls, selling mystic hair combs that nobody wanted.

He gave the basket a little nudge. The basket nudged him back. They did a lot of matey nudging. It was fun.

Joey pointed up and twirled his finger. The basket shot up and spun in the air.

Joey rocked his hand from side to side. The basket rocked too.

Joey gave the basket an appreciative clap. The basket zoomed down to the floor and

commenced noisily banging its handle from side to side.

Joey decided to teach his terrific new friend to play tag. He tapped it on the handle and ran away. The basket charged after him, snapping its handle from side to side. Then it zoomed off, with Joey giggling in hot pursuit! They did this for ages, zooming crazily all around the stalls, sometimes knocking into things and causing a few cross shouts, which they didn't even notice because they were having such a good time.

There was no doubt about it. They were meant for each other.

Their fun and games hadn't gone unnoticed. Other baskets were watching.

'Oi!' shouted the mystic-hair-comb stallholder. 'You there! Stop messin' about and clear off.'

Joey and the basket cleared off . . . but they

didn't stop messing about.

'Is this how I get to the first floor, please?' Sylphine asked breathlessly, peering into the Lift. 'Where the Fearsome Creatures and Exotic Beasts live?'

'This is the Lift to the upper floors, yes, miss,' said a uniformed elf in a pillbox hat. To make up for his tiny size, he had a huge, important-looking ginger moustache that stuck out on either side of his cheeks. He was sitting on a tall stool next to a row of buttons in what looked like an open walk-in cupboard. 'I am Keith, your Elevator Elf. May I ask – is this your first time?'

'Yes. What do I do?'

'Just step in and leave everything to me.'

Nervously, Sylphine squeezed into the small, stuffy cupboard, and her basket followed.

Two doors slid out of the walls and closed behind her. Meaning now she was in a closed small, stuffy cupboard with an elf called Keith, Keith's moustache and a floating basket, in the bottom of which was a spur-of-the-moment selection – a long, fringed, wispy green scarf that Sylphine had spotted on a stall and simply been unable to resist.

Immediately she felt horribly hot. She wished she'd got a fan instead of a scarf.

'Mind the doors, going up!' announced Keith, and pressed a button. There was a pinging noise followed by a purring sound and Sylphine's stomach did a horrible flip.

'Stop,' said Sylphine. 'I'll take the stairs.'

'No stopping between floors, miss,' said Keith.

'Health and safety. Anyway, we're here.'

Sylphine's stomach did a final lunge, then returned to its rightful place. The doors opened.

'First floor! Hall of Mirrors to your right, Menagerie of Fearsome Creatures and Exotic Beasts to your left. Thank you and have a nice day.'

Sylphine stumbled out, trailed by her basket, and the doors closed behind.

She found herself in a red-carpeted corridor and, following Keith's instructions, she turned left. At the end of a long corridor was an archway from which hung a heavy red velvet curtain. Written above in ornate gold letters was a single word that caused her heart to skip a beat.

···•• MENAGERIE ••···

Sylphine didn't think she had ever been more

excited. Crookfinger Forest had its fair share of regular animals, but none that you could call exotic. Imagine how wonderful it would be to have a *magical* pet. One who would follow her round and eat from her hand and pose picturesquely in the background while she did her barefoot moon dancing. Instead of Aggie Wiggins with the Frizzy Hair, she would be known as That Girl with the Unicorn! Yes, it had to be a unicorn. Nothing else would do.

Sylphine practically skipped up to the red curtain, so keen was she to pick out the perfect pet! But pinned to the curtain was a scrawled note in pencil. It said:

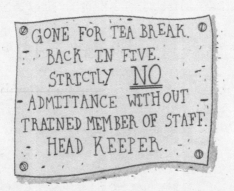

GONE FOR TEA BREAK.
BACK IN FIVE.
STRICTLY <u>NO</u>
ADMITTANCE WITHOUT
TRAINED MEMBER OF STAFF.
HEAD KEEPER.

Not one to be put off by silly notes, Sylphine pulled aside the curtain and stepped in.

The light from the shop faded as the curtain fell closed behind her. In the dimness she could just make out a barred-off area directly ahead, with a latched door. The bars went from floor to ceiling. Behind them, it was gloomy. Here and there were yellow or green glowing lights of different shapes and sizes.

No. Not lights . . . eyes!

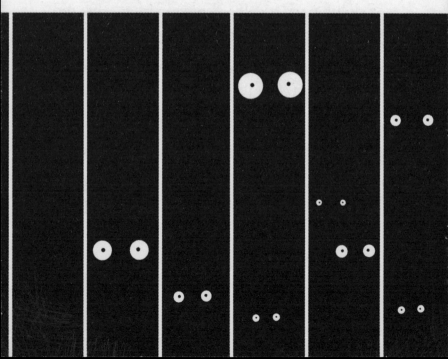

Sylphine approached the bars with great caution. She had plenty of experience of creeping up on woodland animals before jumping out and usually missing. But these animals were Fearsome and Exotic. Easily startled. She had to be extremely careful not to mess up. . .

. . . which was when she tripped over her shoelace and fell into the bars with a loud clang! Instantly, a bright white floodlight came on, brilliantly illuminating the room.

Now that she could see, Sylphine took in the spacious area behind the bars that was obviously designed to accommodate the whims of a selection of assorted magical species in fake natural surroundings. There was a painted tree backdrop and a large fake tree planted slap bang in the middle, its fanciful branches coiling up and reaching out to all sides. A plump golden phoenix sat on a lower branch, which had been kitted out with a feeding tray at one end and a mirror with a bell at the other. In one corner of the enclosure, a small green dragon was curled up on a pretend rock, which showed evidence of smoke damage. The dragon was about the size of a footstool, with stubby little wings.

Small lizard-like creatures peered from the shadows of false logs and clumps of grass. Salamanders, maybe, or perhaps basilisks? Sylphine had heard the names but wasn't sure which was which or even if they were remotely alike. Anyway, they were a bit dull and clearly only there to make up the numbers. Something hulking, white and furry sat in another corner, its feet in a clinking bucket of ice. Could it be a yeti? Maybe. But Sylphine wasn't that interested.

Because there it was.

It stood between a water trough (unsuccessfully disguised as a puddle) and a wheelbarrow of hay. It stared at Sylphine, jaws frozen in the act of eating. It was exactly as you would imagine . . . white, dainty hooves, silky mane, pointed horn.

The perfect unicorn.

'Oh!' whispered Sylphine, clutching the bars. 'Oh, come here, darling! Let me stroke your nose!'

The unicorn's upper lip rolled back, exposing a row of big yellow teeth. It pawed the ground with a dainty hoof. Then, very deliberately, it spat out an unpleasant mouthful of wet hay, which shot through the bars and landed with a splat on Sylphine's foot.

Undeterred and driven by love, Sylphine reached up and unlatched the door.

Corbett was feeling like a newly-hatched fledgling. An empty vial of feather restorer rolled around the bottom of his tiny basket and it had clearly done the trick. He should have waited to open it until after he'd paid, but he'd been too impatient.

Glossy new feathers were growing so quickly you could actually watch them do it. His bald

patches were
sprouting
fluffy, downy
clumps. Not
only was he looking
better but he suddenly
had more energy and
could feel his brain perking up. If another rude
retort was called for, he felt sure he would come
out with something so scathing and witty it
would pass into legend. After feeling rough for
days, he was ready to be part of the action.

He perched on a high girder in the market
hall, looking down on the crowds below. There
was no sign of anyone else from the tower, but
that was all right. Sometimes you didn't need
company.

'*Birds flyin' high . . . you know how I feel,*' warbled

Corbett, in his rusty singing voice. *'Bugs flyin' by*
. . . make a tasty meal. . .'

It felt good to be back doing what birds do
naturally – perching in high places and singing.
If only there was a pigeon to insult, his happiness
would be complete.

'I really should be going,' said Magenta.

Her companions ignored her.

'She seems a nice little thing,' said Wendy
through a mouthful of doughnut. 'That Elsie.'

'Nice doesn't make a witch, though, does it?'
said Maureen, tucking into a large slice of cake.

'Where'd you find her?' asked Shirley, dabbing
up pastry crumbs.

'Her father's got a shop in Smallbridge,' said
Magenta. 'She serves behind the counter.'

'What made you choose a shop girl?' asked Maureen.

'I was thinking that,' said Shirley. 'Funny choice.'

'You're wrong,' said Magenta. 'I had my eye on her for a while. She's got a brain. Prepared to put the work in. And she's particularly good at Customer Service. Pays attention, doesn't pester, finds out what people need and delivers it.'

'The same as witchcraft, really,' observed Maureen.

'Exactly. Of course, there are a great many more rules to Customer Service. Being friendly and working overtime and apologizing for faulty goods and so on. Things I can't be bothered with. Plus, she has the knack.'

Wendy, Maureen and Shirley nodded their

heads. You couldn't argue with the knack.

'When it comes down to it, it's all about charming people,' observed Wendy. Which was quite a wise thing to say, but then, she was.

Shirley picked up Magenta's empty coffee cup and stared into the depths.

'Well, now, look at that! The grounds say you'll meet three old friends today and treat 'em to coffee and cakes! That's very generous of you, Madge. Isn't it, girls?'

'It is,' said Maureen. 'Very kind, I'm sure.'

'Waitress!' called Wendy. 'More coffee and another plate of doughnuts!'

Nuisance lay with his head on his paws in exactly the same spot, just outside the doors of the Sorcerer's Bazaar. He had tripped up a great many customers both coming and going, which was fine by him. It was something to do while he waited for Elsie.

She had been gone quite some time now. He hoped she was all right. She had been too busy to pay him much attention for the last couple of days. Didn't notice his extra waggy tail or his hoping-for-a-sausage face. He was feeling just a little bit sidelined. Not part of things. Not needed. It wasn't good.

Chapter Nine
NOW BACK TO FRANK

'Broomstick, love?' called the broomstick seller as Elsie walked by. 'Lovely bit o' wood, soaked in best flying solution, guaranteed to get you there in double-quick time.'

'Piece of trash,' said Frank. 'Better off taking a ride on yer granny's wooden spoon.'

'What?' said the broomstick seller.

'You heard. It's a crash waiting to happen, that. I wouldn't use it to sweep out the cowshed.'

'Frank,' said Elsie as she hurried them on. 'I really wish you would try and be less rude.'

He had only appeared a short time ago, but already Elsie had had enough of Frank. According to the stories, genies were flashily-dressed, generous beings who specialized in being helpful. Not Frank, though. Frank shuffled around in his horrible old pyjamas, giving out insults the way most people breathe. He made comments about the length of people's noses and criticized their hairstyles. He accused every stallholder of selling overpriced rubbish. He sneered and scoffed and mocked. Elsie really wished she could think of a way to get him back into a mirror . . .

Her mind wandered to when they had arrived at the shop. Hadn't the booming voice mentioned a hall of mirrors?

Maybe she could get him into one of those . . . but how? Magic was out, according to

Magenta – and Elsie only knew three spells anyway. Eggs, frogs and thunderstorms. Not that useful in a getting-the-genie-back-into-a-mirror situation. Could she push him? Unlikely. Frank was small, but he was solid. Maybe she could trick him into it? But that would mean she'd have to think up something really clever because he wasn't a fool.

Wouldn't it be great, though? thought Elsie. *If I could. Just to prove to myself that I can.*

In the meantime, there was nothing for it but to fall back on good old Customer Service Rule Four. Keep them chatting. Show an interest. Ask friendly questions. It usually helped when things got difficult.

'You don't *have* to do it, Frank, do you?' she said, pausing and pretending to examine a tray of fake snakes. 'Tell the truth, I mean.'

'"Course I do. That's the job. I'm a truth-telling mirror genie.'

'But right now you're not *in* a mirror, are you? So why not try being pleasant and kind instead of mean and hurtful? Brighten someone's day instead of making them feel bad? That's what my dad always says.'

She gave a little sigh. Suddenly, she missed her dad. He was so much nicer company than Frank.

'Why should I care what their day's like?' argued Frank.

'Because then yours will be better as well.'

'How d'you make that out?'

'You'll have made a new friend.'

'I don't want new friends. I'm not a friendly person.'

'What a pity. Oh, *look!*' Elsie had spotted the

genie costume stall. Everything was shiny and came in eye-catching colours. Everything was covered with spangles and jewels and sequins. Everything glittered and dazzled and shone.

She hurried over to a display dummy, which was wearing a bright green turban with an enormous red jewel.

'Look at this, Frank. You know, a turban would suit you.'

'That's the last of the big-head sizes,' said the stallholder – a motherly-looking woman who would have looked more at home selling pies rather than fancy genie gear. 'Going to a fancy-dress party, are you? Try it on, love.'

'Nah,' said Frank. 'I don't have a basket.' This was true. Of all the customers in the market hall, Frank was the only one without a basket. Even baskets didn't like him.

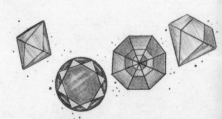

'That doesn't matter,' said Elsie. 'You can use mine. Do you have any money?'

'What d'you think, dough brain? I'm a genie. I have access to caves full of priceless treasure. I can afford a stupid turban.'

'Good. Stand still.' Elsie took the turban off the dummy and placed it on Frank's bald head. 'That looks lovely.'

'Green's your colour, love,' agreed the stallholder. 'Goes with your . . . face.'

'He actually is a genuine genie, you know,' Elsie told the lady. She had spotted a kindred spirit in the stallholder, who clearly knew about Customer Service. 'I know he doesn't look it, but he's the real deal.'

'Is he now? So I can make a wish, then?'

'No, I'm afraid he doesn't do wishes.'

'Funny sort of genie. Where's his

curly moustache?'

'They're not compulsory for mirror genies,' explained Elsie. 'Only the lamp ones have them, he says.'

'He'd look good with a moustache, though, don't you think?' said the stallholder.

'I am here, you know,' said Frank, who had been following the conversation with interest, whilst pretending not to.

'You should take a pair of those baggy pants too, Frank,' said Elsie. 'And the sparkly slippers! It'll be so much nicer than slobbing around in those awf— In your pyjamas.'

'Nothing wrong with my pyjamas,' said Frank. 'They're very comfy to sleep in.' But Elsie noticed that his hand kept straying to the turban on his head. Stroking its satiny folds and fingering the jewel.

'But you're not in bed now, are you?' she said. 'You're up and about, genie-ing. You should at least try and look the part. Am I right?' she appealed to the stallholder.

'She's right,' agreed the stallholder, smoothly picking up her cue. 'You get respect when you've got the right clobber.'

'Please, Frank. I'd love to see you all dressed up,' begged Elsie.

Go on, she thought. *Go on, you know you want to.*

'Step behind the curtain, love,' urged the lady, scooping up armfuls of pants and curly shoes and various glittering odds and ends. 'Try it all on. Just to please your friend.'

'She's not my friend,' said Frank.

But he went behind the curtain. Elsie and the stallholder exchanged knowing little smiles and waited.

While she waited, Elsie was thinking. A plan was forming. Frank needed to enter another mirror. Magic wouldn't work. Neither would force. But she thought she knew another way.

When he reappeared, resplendent in green turban, silver pants, red bolero, curly slippers and a glittering selection of medallions, rings, bangles and ankle chains, both Elsie and the stallholder gave him a little round of applause.

'Oh, sir! What a transformation!' cried the stallholder.

'You're a vision, Frank!' cried Elsie.

'Yeah?' said Frank. For once, he sounded a little bit shy.

'Unbelievable!' said the stallholder. 'Notice how I've right away started calling you "sir" instead of "love"? That's because those clothes command respect. I'll pencil sir on a curly moustache if sir likes. I've got a black crayon here.'

'I dunno . . .'

'Go for it, Frank!' urged Elsie. 'You can always wash it off if it's too much.'

'Go on, then,' said Frank. So the stallholder pencilled him on a curly moustache, using a crayon that wouldn't wash off.

When she was done, Frank turned to Elsie.

'What d'you think?' he enquired gruffly.

'Incredible!' said Elsie. 'You're the geniest-looking genie I've ever seen!' She turned to the stallholder. 'Have you got a mirror,

so he can see himself?'

'I don't,' said the stallholder regretfully. 'I had one earlier, but some silly boy and his basket came running past and it fell over and cracked. But he can go up and look at himself in the Hall of Mirrors on the first floor. They got big, fancy ones up there.'

'Good idea,' said Elsie. 'If you could just write a list of what we've bought, so we can show it when we go to pay.'

Frank stood fingering his new medallions while the stallholder made out the list. He hadn't said anything awful for a few minutes now. Elsie wondered if her little lecture about kindness had had some effect.

'Blimey, look at that handwriting!' said Frank when the stallholder handed over the piece of paper. 'Looks like a spider just crawled

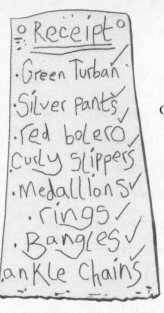

Receipt
- Green Turban ✓
- Silver pants ✓
- red bolero ✓
- Curly slippers ✓
- Medallions ✓
- rings ✓
- Bangles ✓
- ankle chains ✓

out of an inkpot.'

Elsie sighed. There was still work to be done.

'Come on,' she said, tugging his arm. 'Let's go up and find you a mirror. I don't think you should attempt stairs in those curly slippers. We'll take the Lift.'

'Lift to the upper floors,' said the elf with the ginger moustache. He gave a little salute as Elsie and Frank stepped inside. 'I am Keith, your Elevator Elf.'

As they waited for the doors to close, Elsie was surprised to see that her basket was missing. It had nothing in it. Somehow, nothing she had seen had really tempted her. Besides, she had an idea now of what she wanted to take back with her. But it might not fit into a basket.

'Not a lot of room in here, is there?' complained Frank. 'Not with that daft moustache. You could put someone's eye out with that.'

'Take no notice of him, Keith,' said Elsie. 'I think it suits you. '

'Thanks,' said Keith. He looked sideways at Frank. 'At least mine's not drawn on.'

'You got a lot to say for someone who spends his life going up and down in a box,' said Frank.

'Did Mister Glittery speak?' enquired Keith.

'Hah! Insulting a customer! I'm going to complain and get you fired, box boy.'

'Ignore him, Keith,' said Elsie. 'He can't talk, he spends his life in bed.'

'Why doesn't that surprise me?' said Keith.

'Anyway, I do have a life outside the Lift. I see family. I go bowling. I have friends. What floor, miss?'

'First, please,' said Elsie. 'We want to visit the Hall of Mirrors. My friend here wants to see his new outfit.'

'I'm *not* your friend,' growled Frank.

'Mind the doors, going up!' said Keith.

He pressed the button and Elsie's stomach did a flip as the Lift rose.

'Oo-er,' said Frank, turning pale. Green beads of perspiration appeared on his forehead.

'First floor,' said Keith as the Lift stopped and the doors opened. 'Menagerie of Fearsome Creatures and Exotic Beasts to your left. Hall of Mirrors to your right. Do ride with us again. Thank you and have a nice day, miss. Not him, though.'

Elsie and Frank departed the lift and turned right. Ahead lay a tall, silver-painted door with the words *hall of Mirrors* inscribed in curly letters at the top.

Frank leaned against the wall and said, 'I feel queasy. I've gone all hot, look. Why have I gone all hot?'

'It was the Lift,' said Elsie sympathetically. 'I didn't like it much either. Here. Take a hanky.' Elsie always kept a supply of clean hankies handy. It was surprising how often customers burst into tears.

Frank snatched the hanky, took off his turban and mopped his streaming brow. Then he replaced the turban and held out the hanky to Elsie.

'Keep it,' said Elsie kindly.

'Oh. Right. Um . . . thanks,' said Frank.

That was a first, thought Elsie.

'Just rest for a minute,' she said. 'You're still a bit pale.'

Frank said nothing. Elsie leaned against the wall next to him, to be companionable.

'Frank?' she said, after a moment.

'What?'

'What's it like? Behind the mirror, where you live? Genie Land or Mirror World or whatever you call it?'

'It's just a place,' said Frank.

'What's the weather like?'

'Foggy, mostly.'

'Who lives there?'

'Who do you think? Genies.'

'What, lamp genies and mirror genies?'

'And a few common bottle genies. Lamp, mostly. There's only one other mirror genie and I don't like her.'

'Are you sure about that?' said Elsie.

'Yes, she's horrible.'

'Then why have you gone pink? I think you like her.'

'No I don't,' said Frank, who had indeed gone a greeny-purplish colour which didn't go with the turban. 'She's a flatterer. Tells people they look good. I'm a truth teller. I tell 'em they don't. We've got nothing in common. End of.'

'Hmm. What are the lamp genies like?'

'Think they're special. Always showing off, throwing parties with grapes and sherbet and chocolate fountains and stuff. Prancing around in their flash clothes.'

'Well, you'll dazzle them at the next party now,' said Elsie.

'I won't go,' said Frank. 'I never do.'

'What's the other mirror genie's name?' asked Elsie.

'Cheryl.' Frank looked down and traced a little pattern on the floor with the tip of his curly slipper.

'What does she look like?'

'Brown hair,' said Frank. 'Sorta . . . curly.' There was a sheepish tone to his voice that Elsie had never heard before.

'Well, you and Cheryl should go together. Parties are more fun if you're with a friend. Are you feeling better now?'

'A bit,' he said grudgingly.

'Come on, then. Time to take a good look at yourself.'

Chapter Ten
THE HALL OF MIRRORS

The Hall of Mirrors was a vast, echoing space with black and white floor tiles that squeaked when you walked. Shimmering chandeliers hung from the high ceiling. It made Elsie think of ice palaces and wicked queens.

The walls were lined with mirrors of every shape and size. There were wide mirrors, long mirrors, round mirrors, oval mirrors and square mirrors. Some were in ornate frames and hung from chains. Some were huge and obviously expensive. But there were ordinary, humble ones too, with plain wooden frames or no frames at all.

'It must seem funny to you, seeing mirrors from this side,' Elsie said to Frank as they stood in the doorway. 'I mean, you're usually on the other side looking out, aren't you?'

She took him by the shoulders and pushed him in front of the first mirror, which was long and thin with an elegantly carved frame.

'There's you in your new finery. Don't you look nice?'

Frank blinked. He stared. He patted the turban straight and adjusted the position of his many chest medallions. He shuffled around and looked at himself side-on. He sucked in his tummy. He shuffled around and inspected the other side. He turned around and looked over his shoulder. He stepped back. He stepped forward. He moved in close to the mirror's surface and gently fingered his upper lip.

'Do that floaty thing genies do,' suggested Elsie. 'You know. When they sit down in the air with their arms and legs crossed.'

Frank sat in the air and

crossed his arms and legs, genie style.

'Perfect!' Elsie clapped. 'Don't you think?'

'It's all right,' said Frank, bringing his legs down. 'I'm not sure about the moustache.'

'It's better than all right!' cried Elsie. 'It's great! The moustache is perfect! Come on, let's try the next one. Some mirrors are more flattering than others.' She linked arms with Frank and pulled him away.

The second mirror was circular, with a pinkish tinge to the glass and an elaborate golden frame.

'Now, look at that,' said Elsie, staring at their joint reflections. 'See how good this one makes us look? All soft around the edges. My hair's a nicer colour and you look taller, don't you think?'

To her great surprise, a voice came from

behind the glass. It was low and soft, like water bubbling over sunlit rocks.

'Oh, but he does. Although he's already the perfect height. I mean, look at him, the little cutie!'

Frank went purple, then white, then back to reddish green.

'Hghh!' he said. It wasn't so much speech as a sort of strangled croak.

'I take it that's Cheryl?' said Elsie.

'Of course it's me!' purred the voice. 'Oh, Frank. Dear, sweet Frank! Of all the mirrors in all the shops in all the world, you look into mine.'

'Nng,' said Frank.

'But look how handsome you are! I am *loving* the new outfit. And haven't I always said a moustache would suit you? Who's your pretty little friend? Look at her lovely dimples. I'll just bet she's clever too, am I right, sweetheart? And kind. I can see right away how—'

'Yes, thank you, Cheryl,' interrupted Elsie. 'I know it's your job, but that's quite enough flattery. Why are we getting you in sound only? Can't we see you?'

'See *me*?' Cheryl sounded shocked. 'Now, why would you two want to look at little old me when you can be looking at your beautiful selves? I just can't get over seeing you, Frank. It's wonderful that you're up and about. I tried ringing, but you never picked up. Everyone's been asking after you.'

'No, they haven't,' mumbled Frank.

'They have! We all miss you. Especially me.'

'Liar,' said Frank.

'Stop it, Frank,' scolded Elsie.

'But she's a flatterer! I tell the truth. How are we supposed to communicate?'

'Try and meet somewhere in the middle, obviously. You tone down your truth telling and Cheryl tones down her flattery and you'll get on just fine.'

'I keep telling him that!' said Cheryl, in a more normal voice. 'I want him to come along to the next lamp party, but he claims he has nothing to wear.'

'Well, he does now,' said Elsie. 'He'll out-style everyone there.'

'He will. Oh, come home, Frank!' begged Cheryl. 'Come over to mine and I'll make us a curry. I'll invite a few friends round. A lamp or two and a couple of bottles. It'll be fun.'

Now's the time to do it, thought Elsie. *Either it'll work or it won't. Here goes.*

'Think about it, Frank,' she said. She moved closer and put an arm around his shoulders.

'You've had a nice holiday, but there's no place like home. Sleep in your own bed. See Cheryl again. Curry. A chance to shine in your lovely new costume.' She stepped back and opened her arms wide, gesturing at the room. 'Have you ever seen such a selection of mirrors? You can take your pick. Choose yourself a bigger, better one. Or one like the old one. You'll never get another chance like this.'

Do it, she thought. *Go on. Do it.*

There was a long pause while Frank considered. Then . . .

'Okay,' he said.

'Hooray!' squealed Cheryl. 'I'll put the rice on!' And the mirror went silent.

'Go on,' said Elsie. 'Choose your mirror.'

Frank took a leisurely tour of the hall while Elsie watched with her fingers secretly crossed behind her back. She had resorted to the rarely-used Hard Sell and it was a tricky tactic. Her dad had told her to only use it if a dithering customer needed that extra push to buy something that they really should have because it was absolutely right for them. But some customers could be stubborn . . .

Frank was strolling from mirror to mirror, studying his reflection, standing back, stroking his chin and thinking.

'No pressure,' called Elsie, trying to sound calm. 'Take your time.' But inside she was chanting: *Do it, do it, do it, do it do it!*

Finally, Frank halted in front of a mirror that looked identical to his old one – the one that had been broken.

'This'll do,' he said.

'Good choice,' said Elsie. She meant it too. The mirror suited him. It wasn't a flattering mirror. It showed the truth, warts and all. Plus, she was relieved that he hadn't chosen one of the bigger, heavier ones. 'I can just see you in that. So, I guess this is goodbye. Oh – just before you go. I don't suppose there's any chance of you granting me a small wish, is there? It's just that I'd love to know how to vanish and reappear somewhere else. I've noticed how good you are at that.

Would you explain how it's done?'

'No,' said Frank. 'I don't do wishes.'

And he stepped forward and disappeared into the glass without another word. No wish. No goodbye. Not even a thank you. But, like people and leopards, genies don't change overnight.

And the main thing was, Elsie had done what she set out to do. She had got rid of him. That

was something to be proud of.

She punched the air triumphantly and did a little skipping dance.

'Celebrating something?' rasped a voice, and Corbett landed on her shoulder.

'Wow. You look wonderful,' said Elsie. 'Nice and shiny.'

Corbett preened his glossy new feathers a bit, then examined himself in the mirror.

'Yep,' he said. 'Up from my sick perch, looookin' and feeeeeelin' goooood. Top of the world, never better. So what have you been up to? Why the silly dance?'

'I got Frank back into this mirror.' Elsie spoke modestly, but inside she was still hugely pleased with herself.

'You *did?*' Corbett goggled. 'How?'

'I just kind of . . . talked him into it,' said

Elsie. 'Where's everybody else?'

'I don't know about Sylphine, haven't seen her. Magenta's still with the Terrible Three in the café. Joey's down in the market hall messing about with the floating baskets and annoying people. That's why I came to get you, he needs to be sto— What are you doing?'

Elsie had tucked Frank's mirror under her arm. 'I told you. It's got Frank in it.'

'So why take it?'

'He came with the tower. He needs to go back there.'

'You know your trouble?' said Corbett. 'You're too nice to horrible people.'

'Maybe he won't be so horrible now he feels a bit better about himself,' said Elsie. 'Look on the bright side.'

'Dream on,' said Corbett as they emerged

from the Hall of Mirrors and walked towards
the Lift.

'Is it just me?' asked Elsie. 'Or can you smell
burning?'

Seconds later, a siren went off.

Chapter Eleven
MAYHEM IN THE MARKET

Bad things have happened to Sylphine since we left her at the menagerie, about to gatecrash the enclosure of some highly strung Fearsome and Exotic Beasts. To explain the burning and the siren, we need to go back to the moment she entered the cage . . .

Sylphine stepped in, carelessly leaving the door wide open, and made straight for the unicorn, undeterred by the fact that it had just spat on her foot. It needed time to get used to her, that was all.

'Here I am, darling,' cooed Sylphine, holding out a loving hand.

The unicorn lowered its head, snorted and backed as far from the loving hand as possible. Its pointy horn looked unpleasantly sharp.

Sylphine's sudden, unexpected entry into the enclosure in a blaze of dazzling light was also having a strong effect on the other beasts. Over on the rock, the dragon uncurled and started spitting out sparks. The salamanders and basilisk scuttled around in a panic. The yeti opened its eyes and slowly turned its huge, white, furry head. The phoenix flapped its golden wings.

And it wasn't just Sylphine that had caught the creatures' attention. The door to the enclosure banged to and fro invitingly. Freedom beckoned. All the Fearsome and Exotic Beasts were poised for flight. They were just waiting for the right moment.

Unaware of the rising tension, Sylphine continued to sidle closer to the unicorn. 'I've always wanted a unicorn,' she breathed, 'and here you are, so sweet and gentle, the answer to all my dreams . . . *ooooffff*.'

The unicorn had lowered its big, hard head and butted her to one side, sending her flying. Luckily, it hadn't engaged its horn, or the outcome would have been worse. As it was, Sylphine banged into the water puddle/trough and fell heavily to the floor on all fours. Her elbow collided with the wheelbarrow, which keeled over, depositing its load of hay on her head.

Led by the unicorn, the Fearsome and Exotic Beasts wasted no time and bolted through the door, past the red curtain and out into the corridor.

They stampeded, leaped and flapped towards the stairs that led down to the ground floor. The dragon exited last, turning back gleefully to set fire to the curtain.

Sylphine clambered to her feet and stared around the empty enclosure. Smoke drifted in from the burning curtain. She bit her lip.

'Oops,' she said.

Meanwhile down in the market hall, Joey had

been having the time of his life. Watching him fool around with his new basket pal had proved too much for some of the bolder baskets, who dumped all the stuff they were carrying on the floor and came zooming up to join in the fun. And soon the shyer ones had done the same – Joey had become the Pied Piper of baskets!

Joey was ecstatic. He had dozens of baskets to play with now. None were as good his own basket, of course, but they certainly weren't slow. He got them dancing the conga, playing hide-and-seek and doing fly-bys.

Not everyone was happy. The abandoned customers were muttering about poor service and rubbish management.

It was at this point that Corbett had flown up and suggested that it was time to knock it off. But Joey was busy teaching the baskets a complicated aerial dance routine and wouldn't listen. So Corbett flew off to find Elsie to talk some sense into him.

Corbett decided to use the Lift for the novelty of going up without using his wings. Besides, he wanted to say hello to Keith the Elevator Elf, who he had known before there was even a Lift, when Keith's job was just sweeping the stairs.

Which is why he just missed bumping into the wild-eyed bunch of Fearsome and Exotic Beasts that came skittering and sliding and flapping down the

staircase into the market hall, causing more chaos on top of the ongoing basket trouble and the goblin sit-in. People were shouting and complaining. Stalls overturned. A shrill siren was wailing somewhere. One floor up, the smoke from the burning menagerie curtain set off an automatic magical sprinkler system, which set off the market hall sprinkler in sympathy and showered misty rain on all and sundry – a gentle April shower that was actually quite pleasant, although you'd never know it from the fuss people made.

The unicorn, still at the front of the stampede,

barged purposefully across the hall towards the main doors, scattering everyone in its path, all pointy horn and yellow teeth, the very picture of an ill-tempered troublemaker. It wanted to Go Out and it was Going Out. It wanted fresh air, a field, grass to eat and hopefully something or somebody to kick. End of.

Nobody wanted to argue with that. Unicorns were clearly nastier than people thought. Quite thuggish, actually. Well, this one certainly was.

The main doors sensed its approach and began to slide open.

Overhead, the dragon was zooming cheerfully around the market hall, buzzing the odd head, loop-the-looping and occasionally launching streams of sparks to cause small, fairly harmless fires just because it could.

The phoenix flapped up to the rafter where

Corbett had been recently sitting, which was higher than the sprinkler system and so a nice dry spot. The phoenix's name was Phil. He peered happily down at the damp chaos below. He didn't want to go further – this was great. He was out, up, dry and golden. What wasn't there to like?

Well, his name. He didn't much like the name. But that aside, right now, life was all right.

Loud singing being a bird thing, Phil burst into a song about being a pretty bird. He had a much nicer voice than Corbett. Golden tones, you could say. Not such a good song, though.

The salamanders and basilisks, as always, just scuttled and wriggled and got in the way and peered at people with their little beady eyes.

The yeti (Denis, if you really want to know) ambled onwards, getting wet and amiably whacking goblins out of his way, as he made for the main doors that now stood fully open. He was hoping for mountains and snow.

Only the unicorn, named Gloria – yes, they can be girls – stood in Denis's way. She was currently glaring at the doors with suspicion. Automatic doors were a new thing (like stairs, where Gloria had lost control of her legs a bit). She didn't want to be caught if the doors suddenly whizzed together when she was halfway through.

Then, suddenly, there was Sylphine, bursting from the crowd, empty basket floating in her wake. In her hand was the floaty green scarf, the one that caught her eye and somehow ended up in her basket. One end was tied in a loop.

'Mind yourselves,' Sylphine told the crowd. 'Stand back, I'm roping the unicorn in!'

'What, with *that?*' said someone in the crowd.

'No chance,' said someone else.

'Watch me!' cried Sylphine, and threw the makeshift unicorn lasso gamely at Gloria's horn, calling, 'Calm down, darling, Mummy's here!'

The lasso missed by a mile, as everyone knew it would. Caught in a breeze from the open doors, it wafted up into the path of the dragon (Gareth), who happened to be flying by and who set the scarf alight. The sprinkler system turned itself even higher.

And it was then that Elsie arrived on the scene.

Chapter Twelve
SORTING IT OUT

Elsie came hurrying down the stairway, Corbett on her shoulder and the mirror under her arm. (They had used the stairs, because you should never use a lift in the event of fire. Elsie's dad was as hot on fire safety as Customer Service.)

'Oh, my,' croaked Corbett hollowly, staring at the scene below. 'It's got worse. Can you sort it out or shall I go and get Magenta?'

'Sort it out?' said Elsie. 'Just watch me.'

Of course I can sort it out, she thought.

I've got the knack.

Carefully, she propped the mirror to one side, against the banister, cupped her hands round her mouth and shouted, in her loudest, clearest, most commanding voice:

'FREEZE!'

And everyone and everything stopped.

It did. It really did.

The background siren cut off. The sprinkler stopped sprinkling. In fact, it actually froze. The last drops turned into snowflakes that fluttered down and melted harmlessly on the wet floor.

Up on the rafter, Phil didn't flick a feather. The dragon (Gareth) stopped dead and just stayed there, stapled to the air, a surprised expression on its face.

Everybody stopped moving – humans, animals, everyone. Joey's baskets hung motionless in mid-air, still in formation.

Well, they would, wouldn't they? Elsie knew what went into Magenta Sharp's Squeeze 'n' Freezem spray. Nothing except cold water with a pinch of starch. As Magenta had explained, the magic was all about the voice. If you got that right, you didn't even need the spray. Useful hints and suggestions about how to do the voice were printed on the side of the bottle. (Elsie had read them carefully. After all, one of the three rules of witchcraft was to always read the instructions.)

Elsie put two fingers to her mouth and gave a shrill whistle. Down below, all remained quiet and weirdly still. Everyone was waiting for further instructions.

'Nuisance?' she shouted. 'Here, boy.'

Like a rocket, Nuisance landed in the middle

of the open doorway, ears and tail alert, tongue out, ready at last for some action. He looked with interest at the strange frozen scene before him, which would take a human brain a while to work out, but Nuisance was a dog and quick on the uptake. He gave an eager woof.

'In a moment, I'm going to count to three,' Elsie told him. 'Please can you round up the Fearsome and Exotic Beasts and persuade them to go back up to the menagerie? I know you don't like it indoors, but you can go straight back out as soon as they're settled. And I'm really, really sorry I forgot your sausages. I've had a lot on my mind, but that's no excuse. You're the best dog in the world and I've been neglecting you. Am I forgiven?'

Nuisance gave another woof and wagged his tail to show he was up for it and forgave her.

'Thanks,' said Elsie. 'I promise I'll make it up to you.'

'Menagerie up the stairs, turn left,' added Corbett helpfully.

Elsie turned her attention to Joey.

'Joey?'

'Yes?' Joey looked a bit guilty. 'Look, sorry, I know I got carried away, but baskets really love me and I've got them doing all kinds of—'

'There's no time now, tell me later. When I get to three, please get the baskets to quietly and quickly stack themselves up by the door.' She turned to Sylphine. 'I'm sorry, but you can't take the unicorn home, it's too big. It'll vandalize your garden and knock over the bird feeders.'

'I suppose you're right,' replied Sylphine, sounding rather relieved. She had been having second thoughts herself. The unicorn hadn't turned out quite as lovely as she had expected.

'And then,' continued Elsie, 'we're going to find Magenta, pay for our stuff and go straight home. And don't mention any of this to Magenta, because she won't be happy. Is that clear?'

'Clear,' chorused Sylphine and Joey humbly.

Elsie smiled, rather liking being in charge for

once. She raised her voice:

'Ladies and gentlemen, your attention, please. Thank you for your patience. The situation has been resolved. I shall count to three, you will unfreeze and normal service will resume. ONE – TWO – THREE!'

Up on the top floor, Magenta stood in the long queue for the checkout, a small jar of chilly-chilli oil in her basket. The queue stretched back to the far wall. It appeared there was just one elf working on one till.

Impatiently, she tapped her foot. She had only recently escaped from the café and the trio of gabbling witches. She had stopped off briefly to collect the chilly-chilli oil and arrived on the top floor fully expecting that everyone would

be waiting for her at the front of the line, each with a small, cheap item that she had generously offered to pay for. But they weren't, so she was forced to join the queue at the back.

Then she saw them walking in a group towards her. Elsie first, with Corbett on her shoulder, looking cocky with his new feathers. Under Elsie's arm was what looked like the old mirror out of the office.

Next came Sylphine, looking like she had been through quite an ordeal. Face: scarlet. Hair: worse than dishevelled, with added straw. Dress: torn with drooping hem. Shoes: hay spit on one, hoof print on the other. In her basket was something long, wet, torn, scorched and filthy with a knot in it, which may once have been a floaty green scarf.

Joey followed at the rear, trailed closely by a

jaunty-looking wire basket.

All four of the sorry group were wet. Wet and a little bit breathless, with overly innocent faces.

'Where have you been?' snapped Magenta. 'I've been waiting. Why are you wet?'

'Sorry,' said Elsie. 'We all got a bit carried away. So much to see and do. The sprinklers went off for some reason. But there's good news. I got Frank back behind glass, look.'

Proudly she looked down at the mirror.

'Really?' Magenta's eyebrows shot up in surprise. 'How? What spell did you use?'

'No spell,' said Elsie. 'Just a friendly chat.'

'Ah,' said Magenta. 'Customer Service. And what have you two been up to?'

'Not much,' said Sylphine, avoiding Magenta's stare.

'Barely anything,' mumbled Joey.

'I don't believe you. But I also don't really care. I just want to get home. What have you chosen to take back?'

'Well,' said Sylphine, 'I wanted a unicorn, but now I don't. I liked this scarf, but it was – um –

involved in an accident.'

'And you?' Magenta turned to Joey. 'A fake spider, I suppose?'

'I've changed my mind,' said Joey. 'What I really want is this basket. We've sort of . . . bonded. I'll still use the Sack, of course, but the basket will be perfect for carrying the heavier stuff. Right?' Behind him, the basket gave a little bounce of agreement. Both of them stared hopefully at Magenta. Well, the basket had no eyes – but it was staring all right.

'And I'm taking Frank,' said Elsie. 'He chose a genie outfit before he went back in the mirror. We'll have to pay for that too, I'm afraid.'

'So,' said Magenta. 'That's one small jar of chilly-chilli oil, one haunted mirror, one genie outfit, one hopelessly-ruined scarf and one floating wire basket. Strange what you end up buying when you come away without a list.'

'My dad always says that,' agreed Elsie. 'Back in the Emporium, we sell these horrible china clowns. I can't believe they're ever on anybody's list.'

The queue shuffled forward.

'Are you paying for my feather restorer?' Corbett asked Magenta.

'No,' said Magenta.

'Then may dangerous ducks dive-bomb you when you next swim in the pond.'

'Ah, button your beak. I liked you better when you were moulting and didn't talk so much.'

The two of them were back on an old, familiar insult-trading path. Like the queue, it would probably go on for quite some time.

Elsie gave a little sigh. She had had enough of the Sorcerer's Bazaar for one day. It was a fabulous shop in many ways, but in other ways, Pickles' Emporium was better. It was smaller, so there was less to go wrong. The stuff it sold was boring, but it was what people needed. One thing was certain. Her dad would never let a queue this long build up.

Chapter Thirteen
WHAT NEXT?

In Crookfinger Forest, early birds sang in the trees. Corbett was up there somewhere, bossily telling them to move on. This was his patch. He was full of himself now he had a new coat of feathers.

Elsie and Magenta sat at the breakfast table. It was three days after the eventful shopping trip. Time for Elsie to go home. Her basket was packed and ready by the door. Right now, she was tucking into toasted crumpets with strawberry jam. Magenta was sipping tea and looking through the pile of envelopes next to her plate.

Nuisance was snoozing on the doorstep, having just consumed a huge plate of sausages. He had loved the last three days. He and Elsie had spent lots of time together. As well as sausages, there had been biscuits, long walks and a hot, soapy bath!

'Listen to this one,' said Magenta. *"Dear Ms Sharp, I am writing to thank you for your wonderful Belt Up Balm. I have used it very successfully on the goblin next door and for the first time in weeks my husband and I are getting some peace. I have recommended this product to all my friends."* Isn't that nice?'

'Very nice,' said Elsie. 'Just try not to get behind when all her friends put in orders.'

'Mmm. Oh, here's another one. *"Dear Miss Sharp, How can I thank you? Your Yes Drops are truly amazing . . ."'*

Magenta had taken to reading out loud the complimentary letters that were now arriving. It made a nice change to open them, especially ones with money in. She was expecting a letter from the Magic Board any day now about her licence, but she wasn't worried any more. The business was in excellent shape.

'I suppose your friends will be coming to say goodbye,' Magenta asked.

'No. We said goodbye yesterday. Sylphine's having a lie-in because she was out late dancing in the moonlight and Joey's on his post round with his new basket.'

'How's that working out?'

'Good. He's called it Bill. By the way, is there

any sign of Frank yet?'

The mirror was back up in the office. Magenta wasn't too sure about that. But so far, Frank was silent.

'Not a peep,' said Magenta.

'Spending a lot of time around Cheryl's, I reckon,' Elsie said with a smile. She liked the thought of Frank having a friend finally. 'If he shows up and still acts horrible, you can stick a sheet over him.'

'Yes,' said Magenta. 'That'll work, I suppose. Anyway, I'm taking a break from work so I won't be using the office for a while.'

'Not *too* long a break, though,' said Elsie. 'You don't want to let things slip.'

'Maybe, but everyone deserves a holiday. This last week has quite taken it out of me. I expect even you've found it quite tiring.'

'A little, but it's been fun,' said Elsie.

'Hmm. Well, I must say, you've done well. Helping get the mail order sorted. Making up the spells. Moving the tower. Dealing with the genie. Good work.'

This was high praise, coming from Magenta. Inside, Elsie glowed.

'Thanks,' she said. 'There is one thing I've been wishing to know for ages."

'Oh? What is that?'

'How do you vanish?'

'Oh, is that all?' said Magenta. 'Why didn't you ask? It's easy. Us witches call it taking a shortcut. Nothing to it. Once you know the secret mystic word.'

'There's a mystic word?'

'Yes. You just think hard about where you want to go, think the mystic word – don't say it, because it's secret – and, hey presto, you're there. A simple witch trick. You don't want to use it too often, of course.'

'Why not?'

'Because exercise is good for you.'

'Right. So, what's the word?'

Magenta bent down and whispered in her ear.

'That's it?' said Elsie.

'That's it.'

'And if I try it now, it'll work?'

'Of course. Don't be long, though. You need to come back for the basket, and the purse of gold, and the dog. But go on. Try it.'

So Elsie tried it.

Albert Pickles was missing Elsie. He knew that she enjoyed her little breaks in Crookfinger Forest, staying in that weird tower, learning all that mumbly-jumbly stuff. He didn't want to stop her fun. Besides, the Red Witch paid her well and that helped them all. But he missed his daughter.

He hadn't employed anyone to help while Elsie was away and working in the Emporium on his own – well, the time dragged. Customer Service was a bit difficult on your own. Pretending that the customer is always right was so much easier when you could have a good chinwag with Elsie about how wrong they were the minute their back was turned. He thought he might have made a mistake in the accounts too. Upstairs, baby Todd was teething and Arthy and Toby were running rings around their mum. And now, just to add to it all, here was Mrs Scrope, one of his most demanding customers, who always wanted things off the top shelf so he'd have to get out the little stool.

'Is that two shillings you're asking for that fire guard?' asked Mrs Scrope, interrupting his thoughts.

'It is, Mrs Scrope,' said Albert. 'New in this week, guaranteed safe.'

'Guaranteed overpriced, you mean. I want three one-inch nails, a dish mop and a colander. Let me see that red china clown up on the top shelf. And the green one next to it—'

Much to Albert's relief, there came a familiar voice:

'Don't worry, Dad, I'll get them. Hello, Mrs Scrope. How's the world treating you this fine morning?'

'Why, Elsie,' said Albert, 'I didn't see you come in. Good to see you, pet.'

Elsie fetched the little stool and stood on it.

'The red *and* the green, you say?' Carefully, she lifted down two ugly clown ornaments. 'A lot of people are going for these. I'll put them on the counter for you and get your other stuff.'

'I don't know that I want both—'

'Such a good idea to buy both,' interrupted Elise smoothly. 'You're lucky, there's been a run on them and we can't get any more. I think we could do her a special price on two, couldn't we, Dad?'

'We could,' said Albert. 'Pass them over, pet, I'll wrap them up.'

'I can't stop long,' said Elsie, giving her dad a hug when Mrs Scrope had departed. 'I've got a few things I need to pop back to the tower for. I'll be back later, but I thought I'd just drop in to see how you are.'

'I'm fine, thanks, pet.' Albert opened an accounts book and pulled his glasses down his nose. 'And what about you? Did you have a good time?'

'I had a *busy* time,' said Elsie.

'Good, good. Doing what?'

'Well, if you really want to know, I spent the first night tidying and cleaning and writing letters and stocktaking. The second making up magical potions and creams ready for posting.

Corbett was moulting so I looked after him. Then I had to deal with a mean genie who escaped out of a broken mirror. Then I turned a magical wheel in a room full of stars and the tower moved itself to the seventh dimension and we all went on the most bizarre shopping trip. And right now, I'm trying out a wish.'

'Right,' said Albert, nodding vaguely, his nose in the accounts book. Elsie knew that he hadn't heard a word.

'That's about it, really,' she said. 'How have things been back here?'

'It hasn't been a good week,' said her dad. 'We'll be back in the red again at this rate. Although I might have made a . . . miscalculation somehow . . .' He sighed and looked up at Elsie. 'It's just that we spent a fortune on smartening the place up. And your mum would have that new fancy lettering over the door. But does it show?' He glanced around the shop. 'Is this a nice shop, do you think, Elsie?'

'It's *great*,' said Elsie, giving him another hug. 'Just perfect, Dad.'

'Good,' he said with a grin.

'I did have one idea, though . . . What do you think about wire baskets?'

'Eh?'

'Wire baskets. We could put them by the door.

The customers help themselves so we don't have to run round getting everything.'

'Hmm. It's a very modern idea . . . But I suppose we could give it a try. Would the customers take to it, I wonder?'

Albert Pickles carried on running his stubby finger up and down columns of figures.

'Come and check these sums a minute, would you, pet?' he asked.

But Elsie had vanished. Just like that!

She definitely had the knack . . .

Acknowledgements

The terrific team at Simon and Schuster, especially my lovely editor, Jane. My good friend and fantastic literary agent, Caroline Sheldon. My always supportive husband Mo and daughter Ella. All my loyal readers, young and not so young. All the bookshops and libraries who buy this book. The cats who let me cuddle them whenever I get stuck.